COLD RISING

A Cold Rush Novella

ROHAN O'DUILL

Cover design by Rachel A. Rosen.
www.rachelrosen.ca

Interior illustrations by Martin Norr.

www.lowerdeckspress.com

ISBN-13: 978-1-80352-934-9

Dedicated to my sons Sam and Fionn.

COLD RISING

PROLOGUE

Telstat Neptune Station

Josh couldn't believe how stupidly easy it had been to breach Telstat's defences. They were inside the mainframe before the alarm even went off. He had been sceptical about how good the stealth tech on their armoured fighting suits and ship actually was. But so far it appeared to be even better than advertised.

Oberon had the cables hooked up to the access point closest to the evac point and was running the hack. The station's mainframe was a vast piece of equipment: stacks of servers towered around them with mysterious gizmos connected by an impossible number of cables and wires that grew like vines from stack to stack. At the rear of the mainframe, Gimble was guarding the hole they had blown into the side of the station—as it was the only means of escape—while Josh and the rest of his crew watched the one and only door into the mainframe from the cover of two flashing servers.

Josh checked the time. They were sure to be out of there long before any security response appeared. Their intel said it would take the Telstat mechs at least ten minutes to scramble and another two to reach the mainframe. But it was right at that second, while he was reassuring himself how reliable their intel was, that the stomping started. The unmistakable reverberations of a mech squad on the move started trembling through the entire station.

Fuck.

'Looks like our plans have changed, folks,' Josh said, looking up to heaven and sighing in frustration. Why couldn't just one mission go to plan?

'Oberon, you have 120 seconds, and then we pull the plug and get the hell out of here. Everyone on standby for evac.'

'Aye, boss,' the comms answered back in unison. Nobody was taking this mission lightly.

The time ticked down on Josh's feed. 'Thirty seconds,' he warned over the team channel.

'I'm thirty seconds from getting access, never mind finding what we are after,' Oberon replied. 'I need more time, boss.'

Double fuck.

'OK, Boondocks, get ready for a fist fight. Even mechs aren't stupid enough to fire railgun rounds off in here. So we just need to hold them off for an extra minute till we get the goods.'

Josh hoped the words sounded more confident than he felt. Facing off against a company of mechs was a suicide mission at best.

With a massive crack, the armoured mainframe door burst inwards before skidding across the floor, swiftly followed by a flying mech. The mech used directional thrusters to slow its charge and forward-rolled into a standing position.

Triple fuck.

Josh hadn't even known a mech could move like that. Whoever was driving that machine was an ace.

Two more mechs could be seen heading toward the door opening. They had no mods or even a paint job on their suits. They were students, so the ace had to be their teacher, who must have been running a training session. That's how they had got there so fast.

'Oberon?' Josh shouted.

'I need forty more seconds,' Oberon replied.

Fuck, fuck, fuck, fuck.

Ten seconds would have been too much. Josh wondered why he hadn't already bailed on the job. Working full time for a big corp was clearly affecting his intelligence levels.

'I'll take the commander,' Josh said as he slipped between the servers into open view of the enemy mechs. 'The rest of you focus on the plain suits. Let's rumble these soft company fuckers. Remember, you grew up fighting on the streets. Someone had to teach these guys how to fight.'

The words roused a suitable level of angry curses of encouragement through the team channel. The fact that they were about to attack the toughest and most invincible machines ever built didn't bear thinking about. Strike first, worry about being dead later.

Josh was already running at the death machine. He leaped towards the lead mech. It swung its massive right fist on an intercept course with him. It was faster than he had believed possible for such a huge machine.

Josh fired his thrusters and dodged the titanium fist. His new course put him on a collision course with the mech's head. His teacher, Tito, would have been proud of that manoeuvre. Well, she would have if he hadn't blown her up.

The mech dodged last second, and Josh sailed past without managing to scratch the damn thing. He landed on his face but jumped back up into a standing position before anyone saw.

The student mechs had now formed up around their teacher. Josh's crew swarmed the three, which seemed to confuse the behemoth fighting suits for a moment. They were trained to fight other mechs with formations and tactics, while his team of mini-mechs were street brawlers. There was no plan here, just punch, kick and dodge.

Josh's crew got off dozens of shots, but the invincible mechs kept advancing on Oberon's position. Josh had no idea if they were even slowing them down.

Thankfully, Oberon's voice chimed over the comms. 'Fuck me, I found the illegal software. Let's roll.'

'Bug out!' Josh shouted before attacking the lead mech again. He feinted a roundhouse before dropping to the ground and sliding between its legs. His crew evaporated like the proud street scum they were, melting back between the hardware before scarpering for the escape hole. Josh's antics had turned the mechs around. He ducked in between two servers and doubled back to the evac point.

Josh rolled through the hole in the inner hull and raced towards his ship. It was prepped and ready to blast off. They should be safe now. They had cut the hole small enough that a mech shouldn't be able to climb through.

Josh's rear camera showed movement, and—in the most beautifully terrifying display Josh had ever seen—the mech commander came flying cleanly through the hole in the wall. Threading the needle like an Olympic diver nailing a rip entry.

Fuckedy fuck fuck fuck fuck.

This mech was like something out of an action movie. Josh let his shoulder guns auto-target as he dived towards the ship airlock, slapping the cycle button on his way in. The door slammed shut, and the ship launched off.

Josh slumped to the floor inside the airlock. The rest of his crew were in similar positions as the acceleration took hold of their bodies and slammed them against the floor. Oberon had left a little surprise in the Telstat mainframe which should have disabled the station's exterior rail guns and given them a clear getaway. Fingers crossed and all that.

Despite having no other option but to be working out in the Cold, this shit really wasn't worth what Josh was getting paid. He needed to figure out a way to skim something off the top and get the hell out of deep space. If things went on like this, a mission was going to end with a lot of dead people. And one of them could easily be him.

1

Geneva Mega City, 2324

Olgo's two operatives were in play. After countless shitty jobs, dozens of dead bodies and who knows how many servers full of paperwork, Olgo was on a case that could make their career.

Olgo strolled in the shadow of a massive tower block. They patted the black and brown dust from their suit's shoulders. The dust covered everything down on the street. The detritus from the city scrapers far above floated down to the ancient potholed tarmac. Cars used to drive here before personal drones became the preferred mode of transport. Now it was the city's discarded things that gathered here. Olgo could never get used to the smell on the streets. The sewage treatment plants were always at breaking point. Large waste pipes snaked their way through the city, and despite their undamaged appearance they emitted a strange sickly smell, not exactly a shit smell, but something almost worse.

A few people were about, but everyone kept their business to themselves. Masks were standard in the open air. Pollution levels wouldn't kill you, but they weren't good for you either. Olgo watched as the two operatives emerged from the gloom, travelling on foot from Rue de Prince. Olgo's assistants were nearly comical in their appearance. Glebe walked like a robot, arms always stretched out as if to embrace someone. At nearly two metres in height, they were tall for an Earther, and after all the body enhancements and steroids, Glebe weighed about 250 kilograms. To have an operative like Glebe was a statement, and despite their lack of social skills, Glebe was loyal to a fault.

Stevie couldn't be any more different. He strutted up the street like he owned it. Stevie had been brought up rough in a street orphanage—most likely he was a second child, contravening the one-child policy, and abandoned at birth. He had come up hard and bounced around every seedy corner of Geneva. Stevie knew everything there was to know about the underbelly of the city. It seemed impossible to know every lowlife in a metropolis of two hundred million people, but somehow, the operative managed it.

Their first run-in with Stevie was back when Olgo had been an officer in the Geneva police. Stevie had broken into a modder's shop and was making off with thousands of credits worth of implants when he literally tripped up over Olgo while running out the shop door. The prisoner had turned informant to get off the hook, giving away a few locations for Olgo to raid. Stevie's information proved so valuable it fast-tracked Olgo's police career. Five years later, when Olgo had secured the job as a Micron agent and received a budget for two personal operatives, they knew exactly where to go for their first pick. Stevie brought Glebe on board as muscle for Olgo's crew, yet Olgo knew Stevie was by far the more dangerous of the two. But in this line of work, dangerous people were the most valuable to have on your side.

The two operatives approached the shithole pub across the street from where Olgo was lurking. The bouncer on the door lost his arrogant demeanour when Stevie grinned up at him through his scruffy goatee. Stevie had plenty of money to mod his face to something pretty and laser his facial hair. But he'd kept the ugly he had been born with. Olgo secretly admired him for that.

Olgo's own aesthetics were never foremost on their mind. They had their hair lasered to avoid the hassle of looking after it. A shaved head was a standard look for civil servants, helping them blend in among the multitudes. They kept up a mild fitness regime, precisely enough to keep their body functioning correctly with the least amount of unnecessary effort.

Glancing around the dilapidated streets, it was easy to imagine the carefree peoples of Old Earth tramping along these thoroughfares or driving around in gas-guzzling cars. What would those people think of the polluted carcass the Earth had become? Would they care? It didn't matter either way; they were long dead and forgotten. The mega cities that were created after the war weren't all bad. At the start they were probably even positive. The blending of cultures and ethnicities had broken down racial barriers. But humans have a nasty knack of finding new reasons to keep others down.

Olgo shouldn't have much time to kill now. They ambled across the street, waving on a passing dealer who should have known better than to look for business in their direction. Right on cue, a commotion kicked off in the pub. The general murmurings that could be heard from outside rose to an excited roar. The pair must have located Ralf.

Stevie had found tonight's target, a low-level hacker who had somehow stumbled onto some top secret software that the Telstat Corporation developed. Ralf had put the software up for auction on the black web. The bidding war that ensued had got out of hand. The bids were now at a stage where Ralf could not possibly hide the number of credits involved and had reached out for assistance to the more serious criminal elements.

Stevie picked up on the deal within minutes. If this software was real, this could send shock waves through the entire system. Every other company agency would be after it. Olgo was an agent of Micron Corporation, the most powerful company in the system. But Telstat Corp had been snapping at Micron's heels for some time. Getting one over on Telstat was the biggest win you could achieve as a Micron agent.

Olgo moved past the dirt-caked window, which flashed out unreadable neon red letters. They located the emergency exit and concealed themselves in the dark alcove. Every criminal worth their salt scoped the potential escape routes before entering an establishment like this. Right on schedule, the door swung open, and the breath of a hundred drunks and the garbled din of pointless conversations hit Olgo like a tidal wave. Criminals were so predictable in their actions—Olgo's job was almost too easy sometimes. Olgo extended their foot to trip the unsuspecting Ralf. But it was Stevie who careened head over heels onto the dirty pavement as glass shattered behind Olgo's head. Olgo spun around in time to see Ralf dive roll onto the street and straight back up into a standing position, clocking Olgo before sprinting off up the street.

'I thought you said this guy was a hacker?' Olgo said accusingly to Stevie.

'He is, boss. But he must have been something else before that.' Stevie gathered himself and started sprinting after Ralf.

Glebe tottered out from the din of the dive pub, wearing a sullen look that was somehow worse than the gash across their cheek.

'Take my drone,' Olgo said as they swiped their watch, and the single-person transporter swooped down to the street. Glebe stepped inside, and the drone ascended unsteadily with Glebe's weight shifting about inside.

Olgo pulled up the feed from the drone's camera and watched as Glebe piloted the transporter, passing over Stevie's head and closing in on Ralf. Ralf must have heard the whir of the drone as he ducked into the entrance to a slumtower. Stevie reached the entrance and spluttered into his comm, 'Target is climbing the stairs.' Stevie sounded like he had been neglecting his compulsory workout routine.

Glebe turned the drone and smashed it straight through a first-floor window. Olgo watched the now-sideways camera feed as Glebe climbed out of the crashed drone and walked past a family of shocked residents and out into the corridor. Olgo didn't think the company would cover the loss of their personal drone. If Glebe didn't catch this bloody hacker, Olgo would take the cost out of Glebe's wages.

Now there was no way to see what was happening. Olgo followed the pursuit at a walking pace while listening in to the comms of both operators.

'I have cut off the top of the stairwell,' Glebe reported.

'I am following him up. He is trapped between us now,' Stevie replied. 'When I get this guy, I am going to—' Screaming erupted on the other end of the comms. This Ralf character must have a serious background. No one had ever caused Stevie and Glebe this much trouble before, not even the steroid-enhanced twitchers.

Olgo reached the slumtower where the action was taking place. Shards of glass littered the pavement under the gaping hole in the first-floor window. Running footsteps echoed through the dark entrance passage. Olgo hid to the side of the doorway and, as the footsteps approached, extended a foot across the entrance. They were hoping and hoping that this time it wasn't one of their own operatives.

Ralf fell hard, smashing his head into the pavement as he flailed out of control. The suspect lay motionless on the floor. Olgo attached cuffs to Ralf's wrists and checked his vitals.

He was alive, anyway. Probably just a concussion. Stevie and Glebe arrived on the scene, panting and sweating from the altercation.

'If you want something done properly, you have to do it yourself,' Olgo said. 'See you in the Basement.' Olgo swiped for an odour-cab drone. Seconds later, a human-sized pod descended, and Olgo jumped in before it whirred them away to Micron HQ Geneva.

...

Micron's Mspire skyscraper stood shiny and respectable on the banks of what had been the Rhone. All the major corporations had their headquarters in Geneva, and most were within spitting distance of each other. As the oldest and most prestigious firm, Micron had the largest scraper, which stretched two kilometres into the dirty sky.

Many things happened in this one scraper. Down the bottom, the agents had their headquarters. As you ascended, the floors became more and more decadent. Many people in management would never descend below the hundredth floor. The interrogation rooms referred to as the Basement were actually on the third floor. The interior had all the glamour you might associate with an old-fashioned dungeon.

Olgo entered the bleak room. Glebe had placed Ralf at the table with his hands secured in restraints. Dark red stains covered the table's surface, with splatters of who-knew-what on every wall. It would be easy to get a cleaning drone to polish the place up, but Olgo found the atmosphere that the stench of piss, puke and blood created was more conducive to their guests' cooperation. Glebe had strapped the helmet onto Ralf, which disabled any implants he might have, while the tablet scanned through his watch.

'Couple of hundred encrypted files in here, boss. Looks like we will get more than we bargained for.' Stevie grinned.

'That is good news,' Olgo said. 'Anything after the software, you two can split between you.'

'You sure you don't want a taste, boss? We can celebrate down The Shamrock later on?' Stevie said, fishing as usual.

'You are quite alright, Stevie,' Olgo replied.

'It would be no harm to have a bit of fun now and again, boss. Even Ralf here could probably guess you have nothing better going on. You should join us.' Stevie's tone was mocking, and while Olgo didn't really care what other people thought, they needed to ensure they remained in total control of their team.

'I have never crossed the threshold of that establishment, and unless I am required to identify your body there someday, I daresay I never shall. Now, unless you want that demise to be sooner rather than later, I suggest we get down to business.'

Glebe emitted a snort at Stevie's expense, and even Ralf cracked a smile.

'As you say.' Stevie's eyes shot daggers in Glebe's direction.

'Young mister Ralf.' Olgo turned their attention to their prisoner. 'If you would like to remain the owner of a full set of digits, I suggest you decrypt these files for us!'

'Fuck you, spook. I have a deal with the Inagawa. They will fuck you up if they find out you took their software.' Ralf glared at Olgo as drips of spittle shot from his lips.

'Do you know where you are, fella?' Olgo asked rhetorically. 'This is Micron HQ. We are the most powerful company in the system. You cannot scare us with lowlife crime syndicates, can he, Stevie?' Olgo looked up at the villain-esque operative.

'The Inagawa, eh? We had one of theirs in here a couple of weeks back. She is ash in the furnace grates now,' Stevie said, clearly proud of his work.

'You see, Ralf, what seems scary and serious down on the streets loses its fear factor when you have a couple of squads of mech marines in the barracks. I could just click my fingers, and the mechs would wipe out the entire population of a slumtower. The Inagawa wouldn't last ten minutes. So this will be the last time I ask politely. Codes please?' Olgo stood, arms folded.

Ralf held his tongue.

Olgo, restless with the lack of progress, said. 'Fetch me the chisel, if you wouldn't mind, Glebe?'

Glebe placed the chisel and hammer on the table.

'Did you know each finger has more nerves than your leg? Well, you are about to learn that the hard way.'

Olgo picked up the chisel, running their finger over the blade as if checking the sharpness. Not that it was sharp at all. A blunt chisel created far more pain and mess.

'They used to use chisels to craft sculptures out of wood. Now they are most widely used to mutilate. It is sad, when you think about it, that something that used to create beautiful things now just creates pain.'

Ralf was clearly caught up in the production. Sweat glistened on his forehead. His breathing was shallow and ragged. Any attempt at playing the tough guy had seemingly evaporated. Thankfully, Olgo could barely remember what it was like to feel that level of emotion. They handed the chisel to Stevie, who took it gleefully and lined it up on Ralf's baby finger. Stevie brought down the hammer with a practised and precise blow that tore the finger off and barely left a mark on the table.

Ralf howled in pain and squirmed in the restraints, but to no avail. He screamed even louder in agony as Glebe cauterised the wound with a blowtorch.

Olgo could see the fight had left Ralf as the smell of cooking flesh wafted across the room. His bravery had all been huff and puff. Sometimes the toughest ones broke the easiest.

'A baby finger is not particularly valuable, but we will soon get to fingers that you find very useful in your line of work. I suggest you cooperate. Will you input the codes now?'

The prisoner just nodded, sucking in breaths, trying to calm himself.

'Excellent.' Olgo said. 'The next step is finding out exactly how you came into possession of this software. Where did you get it?'

Ralf looked worriedly at Stevie, who was still play-acting with the chisel.

'I used to date this guy, Josh. He was the boss of a gang of mercs I used to roll with. We were called the Boondock Crew.' That would tally with Ralf's ability to evade their operatives.

Olgo looked at Stevie with a raised eyebrow.

'Yeah, I knew a few of them,' Stevie said. 'Pretty professional crew, to give them their due. But they disappeared a couple of years back. Rumour was they got a gig in Mexico.'

It was times like this that Olgo appreciated what a valuable asshole Stevie was.

'Judging from the lag in comms, my guess is they went to the Cold,' Ralf confessed unaided.

'And this Josh fella, he needed you to act as the fence here on Earth?' Olgo asked.

Ralf just nodded.

Who the hell would hire a ragtag bunch of mercs and send them to the Cold at the edge of the Solar system? Greenpeace only dealt with believers. The syndicates couldn't possibly afford a ship, and even if they could, sending mercs up against mechs would not end well for them. There was more to this than just the Telstat software.

'Give him a pain jab so he can get to work, please, Glebe? Let's get this show on the road.'

Stevie fed the files into the tabletop holo and freed one of Ralf's hands so he could type the decryption codes into the files.

Olgo turned to Stevie. 'If that software does prove Telstat was dabbling in AI, this could be our ticket to the big leagues and worth a lot more to us than what you will get for the rest of those files. Make sure you open every single file on that watch. Once I establish which ones we need, you can do what you want with the rest, but I need to review everything first. Ping me when it's done.'

'Sure thing, boss.' The excitement slowly faded from Stevie's face as he realised he would be stuck there for hours, and he might not make it down to the Shamrock at all tonight. But that was of no concern to Olgo. This was their chance to move up the ladder. The Agency's director had taken a dislike to Olgo after they solved a case that the director had put in storage. The resulting imprisonment of the director's sibling had cemented Olgo's fate. But today's discovery would put Olgo on the radar of the board.

'And Stevie,' Olgo whispered as they moved in close. 'No one can know that it was us that got the software, so tie up the loose end.'

Stevie winked at Olgo, the glee returning to his face. Stevie appeared to be developing a level of gratification in murder. Death was a necessary outcome for many situations in their line of work, but relishing the idea of taking a life was a worrying development. In particular, off-duty murders were a bureaucratic nightmare. Olgo would need to keep a closer eye on Stevie.

2

The Pit, Opportunity City, Mars

Suong turned off her watch's alarm and rubbed the sleep from her eyes. Her face was just twenty centimetres below the rock's surface. The dim sidelight bounced all around the roughly hewn basalt tube that was her bedroom. The ever-present drilling vibrations from below felt like a comfort of home. She peered out at the darkness of the cavernous space that started at the mouth of her tube.

Suong worked the early shift. They used Earth time here. Martian time held no relevance, as they were far too deep in the ground for daylight to matter. The pit outside was in total darkness. She shimmied her work trousers on and slid her folding knife into her pocket. She threw her shoes, tied together by their laces, around her neck, pulled herself from her sleeping tube, and started the climb down the ladder. The horizontal bars were worn smooth to the touch, while chips of jagged paint clung to the vertical poles. She passed her sleeping family on the way to the pit floor.

Once she was on the ground, she slipped into her work shoes. She gave her torch a couple of winds and headed for the communal bathroom. A few other lights danced around the pit as the other early workers began their morning ritual. One advantage of being on the first shift was that you didn't have to queue for the latrines or to get a sink to wash in.

After a quick scrub, she headed back to her family's storage cupboard and keyed in the code to open it up. She took out a breakfast bar and a bottle of water and sat at a communal table, staring up at the vast darkness above her as she ate. The vertical mine shaft was two hundred metres in diameter and stretched up farther than the eye could see. Long before Suong had been born, the ore had dried up in this shaft, and the miners had abandoned the pit.

Twenty years ago, a housing crisis had overwhelmed the city above. Families who couldn't afford a flat in the city had moved into the abandoned pit and set up tents. As more and more families had arrived, they had elected a council to make the pit more habitable. Suong's mother, Kimi, had been part of that council. They had gathered a pit tax, put in the bathrooms and air cyclers, and drilled out the sleeping pods. The pods went ten high every two metres around the entire pit wall. Everyone had their own sleeping space, something unheard of in the city above.

Suong had spent the entire twelve years of her life living in the pit, sharing a communal space with three thousand people. She had rarely left until she had started her first job two years earlier.

Now, she worked six hours a day, six days a week. She wasn't allowed to work ten-hour shifts until she was fourteen. While her company didn't follow UN work practices, they had their own rules. She finished up her breakfast and started towards the cage. The first ascent to the city above was at 0430. It was a fifteen-minute ride straight up.

'Wait up, Xuan,' she shouted as she raced up beside her best friend. Xuan smiled at her warmly and patted her on the head as they made their way into the cage together. They found their usual spot on the floor at the back and seated themselves for the ride.

'Where are you working today?' Suong asked.

'Down the main shaft again, boring stuff, just guiding the carts back and forward.'

Xuan worked for a mining company. He was strong for his thirteen years, already resembling a man, handsome with tousled hair that looked like he had styled it rather than just what he had woken up with. He wore a pair of dirty, oversized overalls and big protective safety boots. Suong was jealous that Xuan got to explore down the mining shafts. She felt insignificant beside her friend, with her tight haircut and her child's body. Would she ever grow up and become an adult?

'I don't care what you say. It has to be more interesting than cleaning stupid machines!' Suong worked for a garment manufacturing company. While the machines stopped between shifts, Suong and the other kids on her crew would climb into the machinery's bowels, cleaning the internal components and clearing any blockages. She had wanted to work for a mining company, but she was tiny and weak, and none of them would take her.

'The grass is always greener, as they say,' Xuan said knowingly.

'I've never even seen grass, so how would I know that?' Suong folded her arms sulkily as Xuan just smiled back at her.

They disembarked the cage at the top of the shaft. Suong said goodbye to her friend and made her way to the Newstar factory. She clocked in at the entrance and headed for her locker, where she geared up in the protective clothing. The chemicals they used for cleaning were corrosive, so they needed suits, gloves and masks while they worked inside the machines.

Suong and the other machine rats met Boupha outside the workshop. Boupha was in charge of Suong's crew. She was in her early twenties but had worked at Newstar since she was ten. She was strict and always made sure the rats carried out their duties correctly. But Suong liked her. She instructed every child with meticulous training and was as rigorous about the crews' safety as she was about everything else. Being unscarred in Opportunity City was a rarity, so it was something that Suong could be happy about in her job.

'Line up, kids. You better all have your gear on correctly. If I have to dress you again, Chang, you will be on toilet duty for a month,' Boupha said as she proceeded to check all of their safety gear.

Suong knew the protective gear was for her own welfare, but she detested it. The machines were always hot inside. They could only afford to stop for a minimum of one hour a day between shifts, and the residual heat roasted them as they climbed into the machines. Suong sweated as she toiled with scrubber and polisher, the lenses in her mask fogging up as she overheated in the equipment's guts. At least it was only an hour in hell. Suong played a game every day to see how fast she could get through her section and how quickly she could get out of the machine and move on to the less taxing jobs for the rest of the day.

Boupha checked off their names as they exited the machine. Suong was second out. Only Chang was quicker than her, but she suspected he hadn't cleaned his section properly. Soon, the rest of the crew emerged through the access ports on the machinery. Suddenly, the machine started a tick-ticking that signalled it was starting up. Boupha looked up and let out a roar at the operator who had already begun the startup procedures on the equipment. 'Shut that down now.'

The operator must have been new, as he didn't seem scared of Boupha and ignored her demands.

Boupha looked down at her list. 'Chimak,' Boupha called out loudly over the now clanking equipment. They all looked around. Chimak was nowhere to be seen. Boupha ran at the operative, shoving the much bigger operator out of the way as she hit the emergency stop button.

'Suong, get the medic, quickly,' Boupha shouted as she released the access doors to the machine.

Suong turned and ran as fast as possible through the factory entrance and down the street to the Guild medical centre. The horror of what Boupha might find inside the machine drove her to push past adults and force her way past the crowd in the medical centre foyer. She shouted through ragged breaths at the receptionist. 'Someone is stuck in a machine at Newstar. Please send help quickly.'

The receptionist picked up a phone, and a minute later, two paramedics appeared in the foyer. 'This way,' Suong shouted as she ran back out the doors. The medics followed, walking quickly but refusing to break into a run no matter how much Suong pleaded through teary eyes for them to hurry. Guild workers thought themselves a different class than normal workers and didn't like to be ordered about by the ants.

A crowd had gathered around the machine, and Suong had to push through as she led the medics to the site of the accident.

'Out of the way, let us do our work,' one medic shouted as they kneeled down beside Boupha, who was red in the face, holding an unconscious Chimak in her arms. Suong turned away from the sight; the burns and blisters on Chimak's face were shocking. Suong felt guilty about how glad she was that it wasn't one of her friends. Chimak had been shy, a bit of a loner, and Suong had never paid him much attention. She hoped it looked worse than it was. But then, the bulging blisters and sizzling skin looked worse than anything she could imagine.

Boupha appeared beside her, hands blistered and covered in glistening cooling gel. The same gel gave off a sickening sweet smell that turned Suong's stomach.

'Good work fetching the medics, Suong. Now go take a break with the rest of the crew,' Boupha ordered.

As she shuffled towards the canteen, Suong could hear the plant manager behind her shouting at the operator to get the machine up and running again as he ushered everyone else back to their workstations. As if ten minutes of lost production were more important than a child's life.

The unscheduled break passed slowly in shocked silence. Suong watched the cacophony of emotions in the other children. Terror, love, hate, denial and the worst of all, indifference. What were they being turned into?

Boupha reappeared twenty minutes later and sent them out on the general cleaning duties. Normally, Suong hated the monotony of it, but today she was far too distracted to care. She just wanted to finish up and get back to the pit for a few hours of school before bedtime. She wished she could forget the image of Chimak's face. Just pretend it never happened. The sooner she finished school and went for that scholarship, the better. Today was an incentive to work harder to get off this bloody planet. What kind of place let kids get burnt up inside machines? She was going to get a job on a spaceship. One day she would be a science officer and explore the cosmos. She would head out into the sky that she had never seen.

3

Mspire, Geneva Mega City

Olgo waited patiently outside the Micron boardroom. This was their first time being on the top floor of a scraper, not to mention the city's highest. Micron's CEO was rarely seen these days. She had made it to 120 years old, and the rumour was that, despite being the richest woman in the system, she was struggling to keep herself alive. Science could only do so much. While almost everyone with enough credits modded their body in one way or another, the brain, as Olgo knew only too well, was far beyond humans' ability to replicate or repair. No matter how smart humans thought they were, they were in reality barbarians with fancy gadgets, limited by their frail bodies and unreliable minds.

At least humanity had moved on in some matters. The main one for Olgo being the embracing of all types of gender expression. And during that revolution, those who could afford it had moved away from masculine looks, prettiness becoming valued over the old-fashioned ruggedness. Nowadays, it was only when you visited the slumtowers or went off-world that you met people who sported the rugged looks of Old Earth.

Some people would feel nervous about being up here, but not Olgo. They never felt anxious or felt much at all. Olgo's emcon brainwave control device kept all of that in check. Normally, these devices were used to keep dangerous prisoners under control. Most people wouldn't use an emcon because it impaired one's sex drive. But Olgo had never had a libido to screw with. And the indifference the emcon created meant that no event could penetrate or affect their clear thinking. The stronger the emotion they should feel, the clearer and more astute their mind became. While getting in touch with their own emotions was now an impossibility, reading people became easier. This gave Olgo an edge in their profession, a ruthless efficiency with only one goal: to progress their career.

A somewhat flustered assistant in a navy velvet Gucci suit, which probably cost six month's wages, flapped towards Olgo. They picked up Olgo's employee info signal transmitting from their watch and noted their gender preferences before greeting them. Olgo picked up the return preferences. They had no idea why humans still insisted on using pronouns in this day and age. Humans had an inherent need to put everyone into neat little boxes.

'This way,' the assistant said nervously as she ushered Olgo towards the security check. A dozen bumblebee-sized drones whizzed around Olgo as they scanned every centimetre of their body.

'It's so nice to meet an agent in person,' the assistant said, lying. 'I know you are a big deal down on the lower floors, but just remember you are addressing the bosses today. They don't like to be, eh... talked at. So, you need only speak when spoken to, OK?'

Olgo nodded, memories of boarding school scratching at their brain before being unceremoniously vaporised.

It appeared the assistant was balancing on a tightrope of whom to be more terrified of, Olgo or the bosses. Presumably, not a lot of people who walked the city streets made it up to this part of the building. What would this assistant have made of Stevie?

'You will be great. I can tell you are exceptional at your job,' the assistant blabbered on in an attempt to hide her anxiety.

The security drones finished their scans and, satisfied, allowed the boardroom doors to open. Nine people sat around the polished, U-shaped oak table. Olgo and the assistant waited at the entrance until someone motioned them into the centre of the room. An ornate glass ceiling covered the boardroom, but with a filter that made the sky look blue, like it had before the war. Beautiful plants and greenery surrounded them, reminding Olgo of the time they had visited the botanical garden as a child. This much greenery was a rare thing in Geneva city.

On cue, the assistant spoke up. 'Persons of the board, presenting Agent Olgo, who will deliver a report on the next item on the agenda, illegal Telstat software.'

An elderly lady who could only be Genevieve sat at the head of the table. She swept her hand casually in their direction, and in a surprisingly clear voice declared, 'Proceed.'

Olgo engaged the holo in the centre of the room and a list of bullet-pointed sentences floated beside them. Who doesn't love bullet points in a presentation?

'Two weeks ago, my team captured a stolen piece of Telstat software. On investigation, it would appear that the software has elements of AI in it.'

Gasps and disbelieving utterances swept around the room.

'What is this, China in the 2070s?' a red-faced board member with sweat marks on their white shirt asked incredulously to no one in particular.

In the early 21st century, China implemented a social credit system for their population. After years of scandals involving the politicians that exploited the programme, they decided only AI could run the system without exploitation.

Despite all the fail-safes put in place to prevent it, the AI evolved. Two years later, it took command of every high-tech piece of machinery in the Chinese military. The AI believed that, to bring balance back to Earth, it needed to reduce the human population to under one billion. In the end, as the human armies prevailed, the cornered AI employed bio and nuclear weapons. It turned out the AI was just as self-serving as humanity when it came to the planet's well-being, and they were still dealing with the fallout 250 years later.

'No one would be so stupid. Not after—' Genevieve recoiled and raised her gaze to the ceiling, its deceptive blue filter masking the ruined atmosphere outside. As if she, and everyone around the table, didn't owe their power to the AI Wars having wiped out their nation-state competition and leaving the big corps to run the system. But something was off in her utterances; her movements too choreographed. Olgo could tell the CEO already knew about Telstat's AI software.

Genevieve shushed the rest of the table and, looking at Olgo with disturbingly sharp eyes, continued, 'You said elements of AI, Agent. Please explain what that means.'

Olgo swiped to the next page of their presentation. 'They specifically designed this software to help the fighter pilots of drone ships. The software predicts what the pilot is about to do and steers the ship in that way, milliseconds earlier than the pilot would do in reality. Milliseconds may sound trivial to us. But fighter ships manoeuvre at colossal speeds, so any increase in reaction time in a dogfight is critical, as we witnessed in the latest Cold Rush. Last week in a battle to secure the resources of an exo-asteroid entering the system, Telstat wiped out over thirty enemy Ganges fighters with only a couple of casualties. The software predicts the pilot's decision with 99.6% accuracy. Telstat will insist that this software only supports the pilot's decision-making and doesn't qualify as AI.'

'So, where does that leave us legally?' the CEO asked. Again, a rehearsed question. It would appear that Olgo was inadvertently part of a staged production.

'According to our expert, this software is Artificially Intelligent. However, Telstat has credible evidence that it is purely predicting human behaviour and not making actual decisions. If we bring this to the UN, Telstat will most likely drown them in reports, and that will give the UN reason enough to drag their feet and, more than likely, not take any action.'

The CEO turned to her second-in-command to her right. 'Viable options, Norma?'

Norma looked positively childlike compared to her boss, despite certainly being at least in her seventies. 'We could either give this info to the Ganges Corporation and let them duke it out in court with Telstat, or we could put it in our back pocket and keep it as a bargaining chip for our next skirmish with Telstat.'

The pinpoint eyes of the CEO turned back to Olgo. 'Agent, which option do you think we should take?'

'Neither,' came Olgo's deadpan response, to some murmurings at the table. The suits appeared unhappy that Olgo was being asked their opinion and seemed particularly upset that they seemed to have a view of their own.

One of the other board members piped up. 'This is a meeting of the board, which doesn't include unqualified opinions from the bottom floors.'

Genevieve turned her eyes scathingly towards the speaker.

'Sometimes I feel like the brain pool on the upper floors could do with a little chlorine, although in your case, David, I would probably use cyanide to be sure!' David got back in his box, his mouth hanging slightly open for a moment before regaining his composure.

'Please, Agent Olgo, tell me: what would you do?' Genevieve asked.

Olgo shifted on the spot, not uncomfortable, just undecided about how honest to be in front of these people. The assistant was eyeing them nervously, with a "shut the fuck up" look on her face. The CEO appeared to want their opinion, but she appeared to be the only one who did. It was likely she wouldn't be in this job for much longer. Should Olgo risk the ire of someone else around this table? Someone who could be in the big seat soon. Usually, incoming CEOs swept away the old CEO's people and brought in their own. Despite the possible downsides, Olgo decided it was worth the risk to gamble on the current incumbent. She was old, but she wasn't dead yet.

'I would get our programmers to create a virus within this software, essentially cranking up the AI. We tip off the UN where to monitor the next Cold Rush, preferably through a third party. We use our assets in the Cold to plant the virus in a few Telstat drone ships that will subsequently go rogue during a Cold Rush. The resulting carnage will be direct evidence of Telstat using AI, and the UN will have no option but to prosecute them severely. And as we are not in direct competition with them in the Outer Solar System, it would be difficult to pin any meddling on us.'

The CEO eyed Olgo up. 'I like the way you think, Agent. Your plan would involve many risks, and we do have to think of our responsibility to banish AI forever. You are dismissed. I imagine we will meet again.'

The assistant ushered Olgo from the beautiful room as heated discussions began around the table.

So life on the upper floors was just like the floors below. Politics, backstabbing and bullshit. Olgo couldn't give a shit about the internal politics of the board. They just hoped that they had done enough to get their neck out from underneath their boss's foot.

4

Director Kline was waiting for Olgo at the third floor lift entrance. This didn't bode well.

'I hear they have summoned you to the top floor once again, Agent?' Kline spat in Olgo's direction.

'You are correct,' Olgo replied simply.

'Well, this time you better keep your mouth shut. I heard about your little outburst at the presentation,' Kline said, leaning in close to Olgo in what they could only assume was supposed to be a threatening gesture. Kline's statement was unfair. Olgo had only given their opinion when asked for it, but arguing with Kline was like playing chess with a pigeon. No matter what move you made, he would just knock over all the pieces and shit all over the board.

'I shall only speak when requested to do so,' Olgo said, hoping to end this conversation as soon as possible.

'See that you do, and don't think that this is going to help you climb the ladder, you backstabbing little shit. As long as you work for me, it doesn't matter who your friends are on the top floor,' Kline said with gusto before turning and stomping away.

He really needs to get a hobby, Olgo reflected as the doors of the lift opened.

Olgo reached the specified office on the 423rd floor and buzzed in. After a couple of security drones did their thing, Olgo entered a spacious office ornately decorated.

One entire wall was a window that looked out over the city. Just like the boardroom, the view was highly filtered. The cityscapes colours were not the grimy greys Olgo knew only too well from being out and about in the city. One wall was covered in ancient Chinese artefacts. The war had destroyed so much of that country that these articles were priceless. A life-size clay soldier watched over the room. A rack on another wall contained swords, spears, and bows. A tapestry covered a partition at the back of the room, along with ornate oil paintings of naval battle scenes.

Olgo froze as their gaze settled on a set of spiked manacles. Repressed memories gurgled to the surface of their normally calm mind. Unwanted images of hidden trauma assaulted them from the depths of their psyche. But with practised efficiency they tapped the emcon device nestled behind their ear. The device boosted the brainwave suppressant, and they quickly snapped themself out of the unexpected jolt to their system and pushed their brain back into professional mode.

Aptly, sitting in the middle of all the relics, was Genevieve. Her piercing black eyes would startle most people, but Olgo was not most people.

'Good afternoon, Ser,' Olgo said, dipping their head.

'Please take a seat, Agent.'

Olgo sat opposite, placing their hands on the arms of the chair.

'You have a splendid collection of ancient artefacts,' Olgo noted, feeling the obligation to make small talk before getting down to business. Many people liked to do this for reasons unknown to Olgo.

'They are beautiful, are they not?' asked Genevieve as Olgo nodded to appear polite.

'However,' she continued, 'I don't just keep them here for their beauty or their craftsmanship. I keep all this to remind myself that empires crumble and die! Someday, this empire that I rule over will also die. That is inevitable. For most of my career, I have worked hard to improve our company's position and leave a legacy I could be proud of. But as I near the end, I fear people will judge me harshly. And maybe not only people.' Genevieve craned her neck with some difficulty towards the ceiling. 'Do you believe in a God, Agent Olgo? In a greater power?'

So it was true. The old lady was losing her edge at least and her marbles at worst. But it was probably inappropriate to tell your boss that believing a greater power guided humankind was tantamount to worshipping a schizophrenic, mass-murdering, cancer-causing filicidal maniac.

'I am afraid it is not something that I have had much time to contemplate. My job keeps my mind busy elsewhere,' Olgo said instead.

Genevieve eyed Olgo before she continued.

'At the time of the Roman, British, or Chinese Empires of Old Earth, everyone thought empires were wonderful achievements, the pinnacle of human progression. Well, everyone who benefited from them, anyway. But if you look closer, the lack of any kind of compassion towards the general population is appalling. These empires devised wars, committed genocide, created famines, stripped countries of all their natural resources just for an extra bit of profit, and to what end? So they could be the biggest, the best?'

Olgo shrugged. 'In hindsight, it seems rather pointless. However, we have the benefit of a unique perspective, from a position that we wouldn't be in if those empires had not existed. Progress always has a cost,' Olgo said, pleased the conversation had moved away from religion.

'Indeed, it does, Agent,' she said with a sigh. 'Lately, Mars has been on my conscience. Earth is by no means a utopia, but the underbelly of Mars is a cesspit. We put up with it because those small companies manufacture all our commodities. But I am no longer willing to sit on my hands!' Genevieve lifted and dropped her arm, slapping her desk in what Olgo could only surmise was an attempt at an emphatic slam.

Olgo had never been to Mars, but they had heard the stories and read the reports. When Earth's natural resources had depleted, Mars became the system's industrial centre. Anything in the system that involved manufacturing was based on Mars. The atmosphere was already unbreathable, so pollution was of no concern.

The tech companies had vast stations and shipyards in orbit around Mars, where they processed materials brought up from the surface or dragged from the belts. But down below, in the subterranean metropolises of the planet, thousands of small companies produced everyday goods. Massive underground mining operations exploited the vast quantities of mineral wealth. And below the surface, where tech companies had little or no authority, the Martian Guild controlled the caverns.

Genevieve produced a bottle of Irish whiskey and offered Olgo a glass, which they declined. She poured a measure into her glass and continued her history lecture.

'In the beginning, nobody wanted to live in the underground world. So they emptied Earth's prisons for slave labour and offered all kinds of incentives to other workers. They even paid Martian families to have kids. When they finally reached the workforce required, the Martian population was so used to large families, they kept up the tradition. The subterranean cities grew overpopulated, and lives became cheap. Wages plummeted, and conditions that had been terrible to start with deteriorated further. We have nothing to be proud of, looking back at Martian history.'

'I understood as much, but we have no real presence in the caverns and little sway over what happens down there,' Olgo replied.

'That's where you are wrong, Agent. We are their biggest customer. We could not hold more sway.' She smiled conspiratorially before continuing. 'I have an assignment I would like you to carry out. I have a problem with many of our agents; they are too gung ho and get distracted easily. This job is going to take time and finesse. And most importantly, I need it to happen without bloodshed. I understand there will always be lives lost in your line of work, but I want it kept to an absolute minimum. I will reward your team generously for their efforts, and afterwards I will ensure your career is fast-tracked.'

Olgo knew this mission was probably even more harebrained than their usual assignments, but it meant progression. It meant sidestepping that prick Kline. Life was nothing without progress. They couldn't care less if they had to paint Genevieve's toenails to achieve that.

'Agent, I want you and your team to travel to Mars and ensure the companies there comply with UN rights. Micron employees have excellent working conditions, but we subcontract out nearly all of our small-scale production to local firms. Three months ago, I gave my managers on Mars a twenty per cent budget increase to change our subcontractors' deals. The new deals guarantee they conform with UN employment regulations. Every one of the greedy bastards took the money, paying no attention to the additional clauses. I included some special articles that they were too stupid to understand or they simply ignored. Essentially, we can do whatever we want to them if they don't comply. Your job will be to carry out surprise inspections of these facilities and ascertain if they are compliant. If they are not, you may use any means at your disposal to bring them into line. Your shuttle leaves in two days. Don't let me down. You must understand this mission is very important to me.'

Olgo had researched ways to impress their superiors earlier that day. They might as well try it out.

'It is an honour to be chosen for this mission. Your underprivileged childhood has given you a charitable nature, and your determination to help the poor people of Mars is an inspiration to me. You can trust that I will get this job done.'

Genevieve broke into a chortle. 'Surely you don't believe all that spin. I have extremely good PR people, but did you genuinely think that someone born in a slumtower could climb to the top of this building? I didn't enter this world at the top of the ladder. However, I was born just a few rungs down. The system is rigged, my dear. But someday soon, it will all fall asunder. Just be ready for anything when that day arrives.'

5

Opportunity City, Mars

The stinking mould spores filled Suong's airways. The damp stench of the agri-zone combined with the blue hue of the grow lights screwed up her eyes. She kept a sleeve over her mouth in a pointless attempt to filter the air. She hated this place. Everyone did. But that was why the meetings were held here.

'I don't like it. We should go back,' she said to Xuan, who was striding like he didn't even notice the foul air.

'I told you not to come, but you just can't be left out of anything,' he said with a grumble.

He was right, of course. She shouldn't have come, but curiosity had always been her downfall. As they approached the entrance to the tiny passageway, Suong hoped that the two men standing guard outside would turn them away. But the men were too engrossed in some argument to give them more than a glance as they passed by. Xuan had to turn sideways in places to squeeze through. There was no way that the city's security guards or the owners with their fat bellies would get into this place. A secret place hidden by stench and only allowing the emaciated to gain entrance. A bright light came into view as a cacophony of animated conversations coursed around the cavern ahead.

Suong stared around in wonder at the number of brave workers that had gathered. They would ignore a child in all of this, but they would send a grown-up to the Joy prison city if they caught them attending the underground union.

'You just make sure your mom never finds out about this. She would kick me out of the pit if she knew I brought you here,' Xuan said as his eyes flicked nervously about the cavern. His earlier bravado was shrinking in the space full of disgruntled and hardened union members.

A wiry bald man climbed onto the makeshift podium of old pallets, his head shining brightly under the light as he yelled for the crowd to be quiet. The din gradually subsided, and the man cocked his head to the side and waited for complete silence.

'It swells my heart to see so many of you here. I know the risks you take by simply walking through that passageway.' The orator's voice echoed clearly around the cavern. He disappeared from Suong's view as the crowd in front of her compacted together, as if they were worried they would miss something. Suong and Xuan stayed nervously at the back wall as stragglers continued to emerge and join the crowd in front. 'Only last Wednesday, the black flu afflicted every worker in the Transland plant,' the speaker said with gusto as a cheer arose from the crowd.

'What's the black flu?' Suong asked Xuan, who rolled his eyes before answering.

'It is against the law to strike, so instead workers all go out sick on the same day.'

As the cheer died down, the speaker started up again. 'The next day they turned away the Transland workers from the plant. The Guild brought scabs in from the Joy. They promised the prisoners freedom if they took our lads' jobs.' Hissing and boos erupted from the crowd.

Suong wasn't sure what scabs were. But after Xuan's reaction to her last question, she decided to keep this one for later.

'There is only one way to stop this tyranny. Every worker in this city must go out sick. There isn't enough prisoners in the Joy to fill all our jobs. This will take everyone. Everyone we know and more. Today, it is only you gathered here that knows the truth. Tell everyone that the first day of next month will be black flu day across the entire city.' More cheers erupted from the crowd as others shouted out their support.

Suong was distracted from the din as more and more men emerged from the tiny entrance passageway. The men formed into a group behind the crowd and muttered among themselves, not listening to the speaker. Maybe they had all come together from one factory.

Suong studied them closer. They all sported tattoos on their hands and neck. One man walked behind them, saying something as he passed each of the tattooed men. He had a goatee and a series of purple scars across his right cheek, below an eye socket that sported a large red marble instead of an eyeball. As the man reached the end of the crowd, he stopped and noticed Suong staring at him. He turned towards her and winked his good eye.

'Xuan, something is wrong,' Suong said, pulling at her friend's sleeve.

'Shush,' Xuan said, shrugging her off. He was engrossed by the speech from the pulpit.

The one-eyed man pulled a short metal bar from his pocket and flicked it out so it extended to half a metre. He turned towards the crowd and yelled, 'Let's fuck 'em up, boys.'

The group surged forward into the unsuspecting crowd.

'Scabs, scabs,' was shouted as the tattooed group swung their batons into the people in front of them. The entire cavern broke into a maelstrom of chaos that Suong couldn't begin to follow. Shouting, punching fists, swinging kicks and spraying blood created a scene like something out of a war movie in front of her.

Suong grabbed Xuan by the hand and pulled him towards the tiny passageway, towards escape. Xuan looked like a rat caught in torchlight. But before they got far, he regained his composure and shook her loose before running towards the back of the tattooed gang.

Suong looked on in horror as her friend ran into the chaos. Xuan was big for his age, strong and muscular around the shoulders. But as he ran at the mob, it was clear he was still a child among men. Suong followed slowly. She couldn't leave Xuan behind. Hopefully he would see how futile his attack would be and would turn around and run for it.

But it was not to be. Xuan leaped into the air at full speed and managed to latch himself onto a man's shoulder. The man turned, swinging out his arm and flinging Xuan off. Xuan flew through the air and hit the ground hard, rolling over before coming to a stop just in front of Suong. She ran to his side and knelt over him. 'Are you OK?' she asked.

Xuan appeared intact but winded. He couldn't catch his breath to reply.

'Your little girlfriend ain't going to protect you, you little shit.'

Suong looked up. She hadn't noticed that the big man had left the fighting to pursue Xuan. The man had a snake tattooed up his neck, with the head of the snake drawn around his mouth. The snake smiled down at her as the man raised his bloody baton above his head.

Suong pulled out her pocketknife, flicked it open and slammed it down as hard as she could into the man's foot. Luckily, the man had canvas shoes and not the reinforced boots that most workers wore. The knife sunk all the way through his foot and hit the rock floor underneath. The man let out a growl of a scream as his dropped baton clattered on the stone beside them. He clasped his foot and fell backwards onto his arse as he tried to remove the blade.

'Up now,' Suong yelled at Xuan, dragging the dazed boy to his feet and pulling him as fast as she could behind her. Soon they were flying through the narrow passageway, bashing off the rough outcrops as they went. Once they were out into a main passageway, they sprinted out of the agri-zone. Sucking in the mouldy, spore-filled air was the least of their worries.

As they passed into the central part of the city, Suong pulled Xuan into a small alcove. And they sat, catching their breath.

'We need to tell someone. We need to get help,' Suong said, eyes wide and jaw set determinedly.

'Who we going to tell?' Xuan said, tears streaking down his face. 'Every good guy in this city is back there in that cave, getting the shit kicked out of them.'

6

Micron Mars Station

Olgo couldn't imagine why anyone voluntarily made the two-year journey to Neptune. The eight-week trip to Mars had been bad enough. They were outside the window for the shortest travel between the two planets, but thankfully not at the opposite end of that cycle. The transport ship docked at Micron Mars station, which was as large and ostentatious as one might expect. The interconnecting passengers were jammed into a turbolift, the designer of which had clearly never considered Glebe would be one of its occupants. The lift itself didn't seem affected as it sped them at breakneck speed to a shuttlecraft.

Olgo took a window seat and watched as they departed the rotating station and soon entered the thin Martian atmosphere. Glebe turned grey and looked like they might get to see their breakfast again as the turbulence shook the craft. But they were soon through the worst of it, and the natural gravity took hold of their bodies once again. Portrock City's huge hangar bay doors opened in the red desert as the shuttle approached. Olgo found it difficult to imagine an entire city lay underneath. The only signs were the hundreds of chimneys and filtered vents that poked up through the dirt-strewn rocky terrain.

Olgo and their operatives exited the craft and walked out of the corridor from the shuttle bay into the main terminal. Inside, the port had a high ceiling and was well lit. So far, Mars didn't look as dingy as they had made it out to be. On production of their IDs, a security guard waved them into a separate channel, skipping the security screening area.

They emerged on the other side to find multiple attendants holding holos displaying arriving passenger's names. Glebe spotted their contact among the crowd, and they followed them out of the hustle and bustle towards the light rail station.

'My name is Tasha, she/her. We tend not to transmit our personal data on Mars, and I would advise you to take the same approach. I will be your guide around Portrock City. We have assigned you spacious rooms in the Micron HQ building.'

Tasha was a tall, striking young lady with high cheekbones and none of the typical Martian drawl detectable in her accent. She wore a tight fitting business suit with a red Micron brooch. Presumably they coloured everything red on Mars. Olgo could tell straight away that this was not Tasha's usual job. Micron management on Mars had assigned them somebody competent. Which meant that Tasha was either here to provide the best help possible or to spy on them. As long as the mission was successful, Olgo didn't really care either way. Olgo observed Stevie licking his lips as he watched Tasha lead them to the station. It was never ideal having your operatives around regular people.

'Here is the location where I want to go first.' Olgo swiped a text from their watch over to Tasha's. She looked down at the address with wide eyes and swallowed before replying. 'Eh, would you not prefer to get settled into your lodgings first, Agent?'

'I have spent eight weeks twiddling my thumbs on a spaceship. The sooner we get to work, the sooner we can get off this rock. If you don't have the time to bring us, just point us in the right direction.'

'Of course I'll bring you. It's just we will have to walk most of the way, as the trams go nowhere near this location.'

Olgo sensed she was trying to put them off the idea. Did she have instructions to keep them away from certain places, or was she genuinely surprised by the request? 'I could really do with stretching my legs. Please lead the way,' Olgo said with a forced smile.

Tasha had not been exaggerating when she said their destination was nowhere near the tramlines. At first they had walked through a brightly lit shopping district, with all the animatronic mannequins and welcoming mood lighting that would be standard in any Earth mall. The Martians generally dressed more conservatively than people on Earth. Everyone wore smart suits of greys and blacks with trimmings of red. The well-dressed clientele perused the offerings with soya coffees in hand and Hugo Boss or Cartier shopping bags hanging from their elbows. The only real giveaway that they were on Mars was the polished rock ceiling. But soon, the tunnels shrank and tightened. It was too tight for personal drones, so walking was the only option. Through the years, there had been proposals to build massive glass domes on Mars and even hopes of terraforming to make the atmosphere breathable. But that all cost money and had no significant benefit to the companies that operated on the planet. It was much cheaper and easier just to build underground communities, which left them walking in these constricted passageways. The only thing aboveground was the high-speed train tracks that connected the Metropolis across the planet.

As they moved farther away from the business and shopping district, Tasha became noticeably nervous as her eyes darted from side to side at any sound or movement. At least Olgo now knew Tasha's reason for not wanting to bring them here.

'Were you born here on Mars, Tasha?' Olgo asked, attempting to distract her. They could do without their guide having a panic attack.

'Yes, Martian born and bred.'

'Were you born down here in the Crawls or back there in the bright lights?' Olgo asked, nodding back the way they had come. If they had to keep her talking, they might as well find out who this woman really was.

'I was born back there; few people born in the Crawls get to work back there.'

'And what do you think about that?'

'It is how it is.'

'You don't sound bothered with the conditions of the working class here on Mars. I would have thought someone so young would be more of an idealist,' Olgo said, probing for a reaction.

'Well, being from Earth, you might feel there are injustices here! But it is the way. If we didn't have massive industry here, the whole solar system's economy would collapse, and people would all be out on the streets with no jobs. And here on Mars, it would be even worse. If society breaks down on Mars, we all die!'

'You believe that?'

'It's not speculation. Do you realise how easy it would be to kill an entire city's population on Mars? One major breach and poof, everyone dies. There is always some terrorist group threatening to kill everyone for a better life. How does that even make sense?'

'As soon as you try to make sense of things, you have already lost,' replied Olgo, always ready to not-answer any questions posed to them. They had not been expecting the girl to be so forward, but this was a different planet, and they could not expect the same reactions from these subterranean people as they would get back on Earth.

'So you would leave everything the way it is here on Mars?' Olgo asked.

'No. These people need better living conditions. But for that, they need to start by helping themselves, and I am just sceptical that it is possible,' Tasha replied.

'Well, we are here to make changes. They might not be monumental, but they will help some people.' The mission would help Olgo most of all.

They spent an hour walking through dilapidated alleys full of plastic litter and the rusting carcasses of mining equipment that must have been left where it broke down. Sleeping spaces were carved into every wall and covered by curtains or hanging carpets. Humans seemed to occupy every crevice that had formed or been dug out of the rock, as heads popped out of unexpected places to gawk at their group walking by.

As they reached Olgo's specified destination, a guard blocked their path.

'IDs, please.' The guard seemed slightly unsure of themself.

'Why would anyone need IDs to get into a residential zone?' Olgo asked.

'Eh, for security. It's just, you have to be registered as living here to get in. It is for everyone's safety.'

'What if I want to visit someone?' asked Olgo.

'Why would anyone want to visit this place?' the guard replied, appearing more and more agitated, placing a hand on their taser handle.

'Listen up, fella, I am authorised to go anywhere I want on this planet. I could contact local law enforcement to come and force you to let me in, but it would be quicker to smash your head in, and your fly zapper would be of little use against them,' Olgo said, motioning over their shoulder at Glebe, who was tensing like they were on a first date. 'Alternatively, you could just let us in and avoid all the hassle?'

The guard gulped, eyes wide, weighing up their options. They moved their hand away from the taser and backed into their little cave.

'Excellent decision!' Olgo strode past into the Neza Chalco Zone, the most populated residential area in Portrock City. Olgo had seen poverty on the lower floors of Geneva City, usually homeless people with some form of illness, be it drug, alcohol or tech addiction. But these people, living in caves or under boxes, had jobs. They were all functioning members of a profit-making society, and here they sat huddled together in a stinking tunnel.

The smell was difficult to deal with. It stuck in Olgo's nostrils and to the roof of their mouth. The smell of shit and piss and sweat and mould, all compacted into this tiny passageway. The loud nonstop clanking of the ancient air cyclers completed the all-out assault on the senses.

The occupants were gaunt, their skin ranging from sickly pale to sickly grey. Some might have been transparent if it wasn't for the dirt on their faces. Pimex was the biggest mineral company on the planet. Most of their workers lived here during the few hours they weren't working.

Olgo observed Tasha's mood change. Her arms hugged her body like she was trying to make herself smaller, while her eyes squinted as if stung by the awful smell. She had never been down here, or seen anything like this. Olgo wondered whether she would have the same hard-nosed attitude toward the working class after today.

Olgo's crew was attracting a lot of attention as they picked their way through the overcrowded passageway. It wasn't long before a small group of locals approached them. The person leading them looked old, possibly in their eighties, but then again, maybe not. Leading a life down here could age someone terribly.

'You lot lost?' the leader asked, looking them up and down. Their long white beard had black stains, their eyes milky white in the dim light. Olgo considered how their party must appear to these people. Tasha, possibly the most beautiful person they had ever seen down here, and Glebe, the most dangerous.

'I am exactly where I planned to be. I wanted to meet you and everyone down here,' Olgo announced loudly so that those around could hear.

'We don't so much live down here as exist. You work for Pimex?'

'No, I work for Micron.'

Murmurs rippled back and forth across the crowd.

'Pimex signed a deal with Micron agreeing that they would abide by UN workers' rights. If any of you have been subject to an infringement of these rights, particularly any children under the age of sixteen in employment, I would like you to fill out this online form. I will pass the link around. Please give it to all your co-workers. I cannot guarantee I will fix all of your problems. But I will do my best to change as much as I can,' Olgo said, speaking at the top of their voice.

'Who's saying they don't punish us for fillin' that out?'

'I will keep it anonymous, I assure you. Plus, what punishment could be worse than what you already have?' Olgo waved their hand around them, attempting to pull a compassionate expression.

Excited chatter filled the cavern and spread like a wave into the distance. Olgo moved closer to the elderly leader and swiped the link over to their watch while Glebe and Stevie did the same to the others gathered around.

'Please let everyone know.'

The leader nodded. 'You know, everyone in this hole is going to have a reason to fill that form in. You could have thousands of them by the morning.'

'Oh, I am counting on it.' Olgo gave them a conspiratorial wink as they turned and made their way from the stinking subway.

7

Portrock City, Mars

Olgo surveyed the team of four Martian lawyers, beavering away at their holos. They had been logging the grievance forms for three hours already and were less than ten per cent of the way through them. Human oversight was the blight of the system. Olgo was impatient to be away.

'Can you give me the top figures as you have them so far? I don't need exact numbers yet. That will come later.'

Ling looked up over his archaic glasses, clearly annoyed by Olgo's impatience. Micron's Head of Legal on Mars liked to do things by the books. It would appear Ling may have been born on the wrong planet. 'So far, we have 5,131 grievance forms submitted. We have processed just over five hundred documents. Judging by these numbers, there may be a couple of thousand child workers at Pimex.'

'Anything of particular interest?' Olgo asked.

'We have reports of something that we didn't know: Guild workers are required to register as male or female. Seems like they have been breaking all kinds of laws.'

'This place just keeps getting better and better,' Olgo said, strangely annoyed by the new information.

'Stevie, go fetch our guide. It's time to get our hands dirty.'

'Gladly, boss.' Stevie trotted off happily to find Tasha.

'Ling, you should come along for the show.'

...

Olgo and their collection of companions marched up to the Pimex plant headquarters in a flying V. All they needed now was some dramatic music.

They were past the front door before the security guard knew what was happening. He came after them, shouting, 'Stop!'

'Official business,' Olgo shouted back as they piled into the lift. Glebe pressed the highest number on the illuminated pad, while Stevie held a hacker skeleton key over the access panel. The key did its thing, and a moment later they were on their way to the top floor. The lift doors sprang open and Olgo marched across the company foyer, parting two confused security guards on their way.

'I am here to see Garcia, if you wouldn't mind letting her know,' Olgo said to the receptionist.

'Do you have an appointment?'

'Oh, I'm not that type of visitor. Just tell her there is a Micron agent to see her.'

After Olgo spent five minutes exploring the foyer while Stevie and Glebe played a tag staring competition with the security guards, a woman walked into the foyer. She was short and compact and wore a shiny black suit with a red blouse. Martian fashion didn't have a lot of imagination.

'Director Garcia, I presume?'

The lady nodded with a curt smile.

'I am Agent Olgo. Micron has tasked me with ensuring that our current agreement is being upheld.' Olgo snapped their fingers in Ling's direction, who handed them a paper copy of the agreement.

'So far, we have a list of over five thousand infringements that your company has carried out. More worryingly, it looks like you are employing a lot of underage workers. Micron will not support any company that is not following UN workers' rights. We have made that very clear in this agreement. If you look down at the bottom here, it has your signature on it.' Olgo waved the agreement in the shocked woman's face.

After a moment of stunned silence, she finally found her voice. 'Maybe we could continue this in my office with some refreshments?'

'I am a busy person. I have a planet to bring to heel. We can continue this on the workshop floor. Let's go!' Olgo gestured towards the lift.

'The floor is too dangerous. You wouldn't want to go down there.' Garcia backed away from Olgo.

'Too dangerous for us, yet OK for kids? How wonderful! I tell you what, you can either walk at my side or they will carry you. Your choice.'

Garcia turned to run, shouting for security. But Stevie had slipped around behind her during the scene and was on hand to grab her and push her roughly back towards the lift. Glebe advanced towards the two security guards who had pulled out their tasers and were bravely holding their ground. One guard jabbed Glebe's extended arm with the taser. Glebe grabbed the device and snapped it in two, the shock barely registering with the giant. The guards looked at each other before scarpering—smart!

'If you wouldn't mind, Glebe?' Olgo said, nodding towards Garcia. Glebe picked the lady up like a sack of soya and threw her over their shoulder.

Tasha and Ling stood rooted to the spot while all of this was taking place.

'Come along, you two. You don't want to miss all the fun.'

Olgo motioned the two Martians into the lift. 'Factory floor, please!' Olgo was getting a feel for this assignment.

...

One week in Portrock City, and Olgo had visited all the major companies. They had been to plush offices and penthouse apartments as well as the death-trap factories and the City's slums. Slowly but surely, the companies fell into line. How much they were complying was debatable, but Olgo's job was to get them in order, and as long as that's how it appeared, that was all that mattered.

Olgo woke on the seventh day to find a message waiting for them on their holo.

Unfortunately, live holo chats with Earth were impossible. Messages could only travel at light speed, meaning anything between a three- to twenty-minute delay in transmissions between Earth and Mars.

Olgo opened the message. The ancient CEO took shape in front of them. 'Congratulations on your work so far, Agent. You have created quite a stir on Mars. Our office is working through a mountain of correspondence due to your handiwork. And whatever methods you are employing, they seem to be effective. The Guild wants to meet and start negotiations. It was bound to happen, but I could not have foreseen it happening so soon. If we can get a deal made with the Guild, they will carry out our work for us. I have sent you a list of concessions I am willing to make to get a deal done. But do not concede to anything outside of my list. Last, a word of warning. Portrock is the most civilised city on that planet. Do not expect the other cities to react so well to your methods. Good luck, Agent Olgo. May God show you the path!'

Olgo let out a sigh while staring thoughtfully at the frozen image of Genevieve. The Martian Guild, it would appear, did not have the backbone they expected.

Mystery surrounded the Guild. Olgo didn't like things they couldn't quantify or understand. The organisation appeared to be a combination of the English House of Lords and the Freemasons of Old Earth. Only owners could stand for election or vote. The Martian Mafia would probably be a more apt description for them, as they met in secret and had no accountability for their actions. And unlike the Freemasons, it wasn't just the mystery and secrecy that gave them power. They appeared to have absolute control and influence on Mars. A total lack of government or local authorities on the planet had led to a power vacuum, with individual Guild members secretly running each of the Cities. Many of the Martian population believed they ruled through satanic rituals and sacrifices. Working in underground pits was bound to bring the devil closer to one's life. Olgo guessed that their true workings were more likely to be akin to the Gestapo or KGB.

...

Olgo sat languidly on a very comfortable chair at the UN boardroom table. The Portrock UN building was disappointingly small and shabby. It was apparent the UN was not as interested in the Martian underground metropolis as it was in other parts of the Solar System. Not enough big money here. The Tech companies' operations on the planet were minimal. They mostly amounted to purchasing and finance offices that dealt with the smaller Martian manufacturing companies.

The Guild had invited Olgo to meet in their far superior building across the City, but Olgo had insisted on a neutral venue. Then shown up an hour early to appear like they were hosting the meeting.

Olgo brought Ling along for the negotiations. Olgo didn't think they would need the lawyer, but the Guild was sending two people, so they had to even the odds, and they couldn't rely on Glebe or Stevie not to kill one of the Guild members if things got heated.

The UN Director-General of Mars escorted the Guild delegation into the boardroom. Olgo found the UN representative's current predicament interesting. They conjectured most people would feel sorry for the woman. She was supposedly the most powerful person on the planet, but at this moment, she was probably the least powerful person in the room.

The Director-General introduced the first person as Lisin. Olgo had a file on this man, not because he was part of the Guild, but because he was supposed to be the richest person on the planet. Lisin was a tall, skinny man with an officious look and expensive clothing. Behind Lisin bustled in Garcia, the very first person Olgo had humiliated on Mars. This didn't bode well.

Lisin was the owner of a large mining company in Sojourner City, along with a string of other businesses. Presumably being rich was what got you the Chair of the Guild Council. The Director-General began to introduce Garcia, but the irritated Guild member interrupted her.

'They know well who I am. You can leave now,' Garcia snarled at the UN representative, who backed out of the room with wide, darting eyes.

'Welcome to our planet, Agent Olgo. I hope you are surviving OK in our underground world,' Lisin said, starting the formalities with his sombre Martian drawl.

'I have found it most agreeable. I thank you for your hospitality.' Olgo smiled back at the pair, playing along.

Garcia struggled to hide her scowl. The wounds from the humiliating jaunt around her company's shop-floor were clearly still playing on her mind.

'I am here as a direct representative of the CEO of Micron. I am sure you know what that means. However, I understand very little about the Guild and who you truly represent, so before we get down to negotiations, I will need more information about who we are signing a deal with,' Olgo said, addressing Lisin. Garcia, presumably, was a lost cause.

'I am afraid that would be impossible, Agent. The Guild represents Mars. That is all you need to know. I am sure you understand—being an agent, you must have plenty of secrets of your own,' Lisin replied, speaking carefully and clearly.

This was someone Olgo could not easily manipulate.

'In this scenario, you can forget about the fact that I am an agent. I am here on behalf of Genevieve, the Micron CEO, and she has granted me the power to approve any deal we may come up with. I must come back to the point that I don't know if you are negotiating on behalf of Mary and Johnny who live down the road or a cooperative that represents the entire planet. How could I conceivably approve a deal when I don't even know who you are?' Olgo growled the last part of the sentence and narrowed their eyes, attempting to appear irate.

Lisin eyeballed the agent from across the table. 'I can give you a list of all the companies that we represent. Will that suffice, Agent?'

'That will do for a start.'

'Before we continue, I require a personal apology,' Garcia interrupted as Lisin let out a sigh.

'Oh, of course,' Olgo said with a smile. 'I am so sorry for any inconvenience I may have caused you.' It was one advantage of not giving a shit about what anyone thought of you. But Olgo's pandering didn't seem to appease Garcia at all, as her face reddened with anger.

Lisin laid a hand across her arm. 'Thank you for your apology, Agent. Now, we are happy to enforce all the current contracts, bringing all of Mars in line with UN work standards. In exchange, the Guild will require permission to build a station in orbit.'

'I think you may have come to the wrong meeting,' Olgo replied, shocked by the enormity of the ask. 'We are here to discuss working conditions on Mars, not astropolitics.'

'Obviously, you can't sign off on it today. But we want to get the ball rolling on a Guild station,' Lisin said confidently.

'That is so far off what I may negotiate that you might as well be asking for mining rights for the sun.'

'So it is not even on the table?' Lisin asked, the briefest flash of anger in his eyes.

'On the table? Definitely not,' Olgo said. 'Could it ever happen? Not in our lifetime. You want to negotiate, you have to be realistic.' Who the hell did these people think they were?

'You don't know who you are fucking with!' Lisin said, the calm demeanor well and truly broken now.

'Hence my first question to you,' Olgo said, adding petrol to the fire. But sometimes when you are a smart arse, you just can't help yourself.

'Hopefully, the next person they send will have the decency to start a negotiation. Goodbye, Agent Olgo.' The two Martians stood up and stormed out of the room.

Olgo turned to Ling. 'That was a lot shorter than I would have imagined. Is everybody in the Guild as nuts as those two? Do they realise what they are asking for? The corporations would rather nuke Mars than let them have a station.'

Ling just shrugged.

'Don't worry. They will see sense soon enough.' Olgo gave Ling a reassuring pat on the back as the lawyer's head nodded in a way that did not seem to convey his agreement.

8

Opportunity City, Mars

Suong sat in her usual place in the cage beside Xuan, on her way to another day of cleaning looms. But it didn't feel like any ordinary day. Excitement buzzed around the cage, as if the atmosphere couldn't escape through the chicken wire surrounding the ancient contraption. Suong clenched her jaw, trying to pop her ears as the cage was pulled from the depths through the massive mine shaft, grating and sparking off the rocky walls as it went.

The mood had changed in both the City above and the pit below in recent days. As news of the Breaker filtered through from Portrock City, people dared to dream. A nervous optimism had infected the population. You had to be brave to have hope. If it was all a lie, the disappointment would be devastating.

'I am telling you, the Breaker is arriving today in Central Circle at 1830,' Xuan said.

Suong just looked at him sceptically.

'It's true. I overheard my parents talking about it. Lots of people are planning a welcoming party. I am not going to miss it. You have to come too!'

'My mother would never let me go, plus we will miss school.'

'Well, we can just stay in the City after work. That way, your mother can't tell you not to go. This will be the most historical event in all of our lives, and you would miss that for school?'

Xuan was making some good points. Suong considered his proposal.

'I guess I would like to see her.'

'Her? The Breaker is a man!' Xuan scoffed.

'I heard the Breaker was a beautiful Martian woman called Tanya,' Suong stated indignantly as she narrowed her eyes at Xuan, who was being so sure of himself.

Xuan backtracked a little under Suong's scowl.

'No, the woman is his cyborg bodyguard,' Xuan declared, his voice rising with his excitement. 'The Breaker is a giant Earther whose real name is Glen. He is as big as a rock breaker—hence the name—and he can crush a person's skull with one bare hand! If the managers don't do what they are told, he carries them through the factory and leaves them at the workers' mercy until they comply.'

'You are both wrong,' an older teenager interrupted from across the cage. 'The Breaker is neither man nor woman.

They are not big or small. They are just the Breaker. They have a single purpose! A mission to free us from oppression and enforce our rights. Rights and laws that are taken for granted in every other part of the system. Today will be our day of deliverance!' the teen proclaimed as if speaking from a pulpit.

Murmurs and excited chatter struck up around the cage as the power in the words sent electricity coursing through Suong's body. She turned to Xuan. 'I'll meet you after work. We will have to hide out in the tunnels until 1830.'

'I know just the place,' Xuan said with a smile, their earlier disagreement now swept away by the anticipation of the day to come.

Suong clocked in and geared up like any other working day, but the time dragged on. It felt like the longest day she had ever experienced as she longed for the bell that signalled the end of her shift to ring out. Inside the machine, her work was a blur. The usual tediousness of scouring every surface and getting into every nook and cranny seemed to be multiplied tenfold. She daydreamed as she scrubbed the grubby toilets in the changing rooms. What endless possibilities would the Breaker bring to their lives?

Her daydreaming earned her a telling off from Boupha as she clumsily spilt mop water beside a machine.

'The Breaker hasn't arrived yet, child, so don't get ahead of yourself. Keep your mind on the job. If you get electrocuted from that spill and die, the Breaker won't be much use to you then, will they?'

But for once Suong didn't care what Boupha said to her. Suong thought back to the day she had met Mua, the daughter of the owner of Newstar at the Martian Golden Day celebrations. Mua was of a similar age to Suong and wore a dress with beautiful pink flowers drawn all over it, her long hair braided into an intricate design of knotwork. Suong had been hypnotised by the girl's dress and had asked Mua if she could touch the material, as it was nothing like what they produced at Newstar. But Mua had looked at Suong like she carried the plague and replied, 'Ew, you are gross. Get away from me before I tell my father you touched me.' Suong had been infuriated by Mua's rudeness, but had turned away and fled in fear. Those words were forever etched in her mind. Later that day, after fuming over Mua's belittling, she promised herself that someday she would own a dress.

As she scrubbed, she dreamed of all the things that she could do and buy if she earned as much as minimum credits. She could save up enough to go to one of the Tech Academies. She could buy food that wasn't kibble. If she could get a job with one of the Tech Giants, her parents could retire someday. The opportunities would be endless. This was a new day!

7

Opportunity City, Mars

Olgo looked out of the plate-glass window at the Martian surface's red-black landscape as the train zipped along the raised tracks. There were parts of Earth that were this barren, so the scenery didn't look so alien to their eyes.

So far, Olgo hated the desolate planet far less than they had thought they would. There was a simplicity to life on Mars that Olgo could appreciate. Wrong and right were much clearer here, far more so than the usual legally grey areas they operated in on Earth. Their only setback so far had been failing to make a deal with the Guild, but maybe the Guild didn't have the influence they claimed on the planet. Judging by their negotiation meeting, they were certainly delusional.

Olgo was experiencing peculiar sensations about their work on Mars. Perceptions that might have had an emotional element. Maybe enjoyment? Olgo's brainwave controller should make that impossible. But this underground world had stirred something inside them. Whether those feelings were genuine, Olgo was unsure. Maybe it was merely the clarity of their mission on Mars.

Portrock City had crumbled to their will like a soggy biscuit. Olgo had thought they would need many weeks or even months to get all the companies in line. After a couple of weeks, all the major players agreed to enforce the laws, in principle at least. The smaller companies folded quickly after that.

As always, in these situations, a few stubborn owners refused to get the message. Glebe and Stevie had taken care of them in the after-hours. Stevie was particularly adept at convincing people to commit suicide, meaning Olgo was keeping their word to Genevieve for the most part. The companies' inheritors had been much more cooperative than the recently deceased.

Tasha had slowly become a believer in "the cause," as she liked to refer to it. She had even asked to continue with them on their journey across the planet. It suited Olgo to take her along. It was possible to have a much more sophisticated conversation with the young Martian than with Stevie. Glebe never was much of a talker, so her addition vastly improved the refinement of the group. Olgo had also found the woman very effective in certain situations. Sometimes a friendly smile was a far easier way to open a door than Glebe's battering ram of a shoulder.

Tasha sat across the aisle, chewing distractedly on her well-worn stylus as she worked her way through the lists of companies in Opportunity City. Olgo looked across at her. 'So, where do we start?'

'It is hard to say! The mining companies have the worst records with safety and deaths. However, there are many garment companies that employ children almost exclusively, if these reports are to be believed. We have no offices in Opportunity, so up-to-date information is lacking. My guess would be that conditions are actually far worse than back in Portrock.' Tasha screwed up her face as she continued to swipe through the files, using her stylus like a conductor's baton.

'Are you a fan of classical music?' Olgo asked.

Tasha looked at them questioningly. Olgo mimicked her conductor movements.

'Ah, a lifetime of playing violin,' she said. 'Old habits die hard.'

'Indeed.' Olgo placed their hands together a few centimetres in front of their face, tapping their fingers together, deep in thought. 'What little intel I could access from our files would agree with your conclusions,' Olgo said out loud, but was as much talking to themself as anyone else. 'With none of the companies having a presence there, the violation of UN law is likely to be far more open than in Portrock City. I chose Opportunity next as it is a stronghold of The Guild. If we can break Opportunity, we can break the rest of the planet. That presents its own problems. We can expect to encounter much more opposition this time around.'

'They also know about us! You have become somewhat of a legend on this planet already!' Tasha responded.

'Oh, they don't really know about us,' Olgo said. 'I have no idea where the whispers of this Breaker character have come from, but that is not me or us. But it may help with our mission if we can harness that idea. It has the potential to turn into a movement in its own right.'

'We shall see,' Tasha replied, her tone doubtful.

After the tedious process of passing through the train-line seals that kept the underground oxygen from escaping, the train pulled slowly into Central Station. It was immediately apparent the station was on security alert. No surprise visit like the first time around.

A heavily armoured and armed security guard met them as they disembarked the train. Olgo noticed the guard's insignia was covered up. This, along with the balaclava they sported, was a troubling development. Olgo gave Glebe and Stevie a look they knew well. Be ready for anything!

But the guard didn't try to turn them away.

'Ser, a large crowd has gathered in the Circle outside. We have an armoured truck ready to get you to your hotel,' the guard said matter-of-factly.

'Why is there a crowd gathered outside?' Olgo asked.

'To see the person they call the Breaker,' the guard spat out. *Clearly, not my biggest fan,* Olgo thought.

'If they are here to see the Breaker, then surely we are not in harm's way, and my security would be adequate to get me through to the hotel?'

'We have reports that a local terrorist cell is working on a plan to kidnap you. The Guild would like to ensure your safety,' the guard said while eyeing Glebe and subconsciously tapping their trigger finger along the barrel of the bolt-gun.

So the Guild had supplied the extra security. Had they also been the ones to leak their arrival to the population? The whole situation smacked of a setup. Olgo should probably have got back on the train. But surely no one would be stupid enough to take on Micron. It must be just a show, a power play for a better negotiating position. Olgo had no intention of allowing these people to intimidate them. But if they let Stevie and Glebe off the leash, the station would turn into a bloodbath.

'Please come with us before things escalate,' the guard said impatiently as Olgo felt Stevie getting closer and closer to their shoulder. The guard's eyes kept flashing up to Glebe and back again. Glebe was such a great distraction. Stevie would have a knife through your throat long before Glebe could even lift those giant fists.

'I appreciate your help. Please lead the way,' Olgo said with a forced smile, de-escalating the situation.

As the group emerged from the station exit, a maelstrom of chaos met them. A cheer erupted from the thousands of people jammed into the Circle outside. Some had placards with hand-painted signs of, "Break our chains," and, "The Breaker will lead the way."

'Looks like you're the Hero of Canton, boss,' Stevie sniggered. Olgo ignored him. There were more important things to focus on.

Olgo examined the situation as a couple of hundred armed guards held the surging crowd back from the station. The guards were all armed and wearing riot gear, but so far, their weapons remained in their holsters. Martians considered standard projectile weapons dangerous in the rock tunnels, even to the person using them. The weapons of choice were tasers and bolt-guns, which were both only effective at close range, but then everything was close range on Mars.

A military-style truck sat waiting for them, and guards held back the crowd on either side of the small space between the truck doors. But the only way the truck could leave would be through that crowd.

'Quickly, now,' the chief guard shouted over the din as they were led into the back of the vehicle. The inside of the truck was rusted grey and stank of piss. This vehicle was normally used to imprison people. Today it was being used to keep people out. At least, Olgo hoped so.

They sat on benches on either side of the cab as they pulled off, making slow lurching progress through the crowd. The original celebratory tone of the crowd faltered as they heard shouting and booing through the truck's armour. Did the crowd think they were being arrested? Were they being arrested? People banged on the sides of the vehicle, and then the truck lurched as they ran over something. Probably a body, but there was no way to know for sure.

10

The bell finally rang out over the intercom. Suong raced out of the Newstar factory towards the mining pit where Xuan would finish up soon.

Xuan strolled through the gates with five other boys his age. He looked slightly awkward on seeing Suong, but she didn't care. Xuan introduced her to the rest of his crew.

'We are all going to see the Breaker arrive,' Xuan explained.

Two of the boys were friendly and smiled at Suong. The others were either shy or rude, as they barely acknowledged her. Suong was used to that. She was twelve years old, but she was so small she could have passed for eight, and most adults and older kids ignored eight-year-olds.

Xuan led her and the other boys through a dive part of the City; not that it looked any different to anywhere else, it was just that few people were brave enough to walk here. Suong soon realised what the smell was that stuck in her nose as they walked past an incineration plant. The tunnel lighting was sparse here, with bubbles of illumination interrupting the darkness only every hundred metres. Graffiti covered the walls, not that there was enough illumination to read the writing. But she could see enough that it created an atmosphere of dereliction and the possibility of being in danger from the Shadows.

After another five minutes walking uphill, they came to a small hole about two metres up in one of the tunnel walls. They would have missed it if Xuan hadn't known it was there.

'Follow me,' Xuan said as he found some small indentations on the rock and shimmied up to the hole, disappearing over the ledge. One of the friendly boys gestured for Suong to go next, and she scaled the face in a few seconds and followed Xuan down the tiny shaft. Xuan was crawling ahead of her, but Suong was small enough to walk along crouched over.

Xuan and the other boys lit the way with the lights on their helmets. After five minutes, at a crawling pace, they came out into what must have been an immense cavern. Xuan put an arm out to hold everyone back before he took off his backpack and pulled out a lantern. He placed it on the rocky ground and lit it up.

Suong's jaw dropped open in awe. She had never seen anything like this before.

The cavern was huge, vaster than the pit, she guessed. The rest of the cave floor was perfectly smooth. It was a giant underground lake. One boy picked up a stone and threw it towards the water, making a massive splash. Suong walked to the edge and looked in. 'How deep is it?' she asked.

'I don't know. I can't swim,' Xuan replied, shrugging. The other boys had all taken to throwing stones in the water now. A fierce competition began over who could throw the farthest. This brought the shy boys out of themselves as they joined in with shouts and cheers whenever someone had a long shot.

Suong took off her shoes and, sitting on the rock edge, dangled her feet over the lip and into the water. It was icy cold and sent a shock through her body. The skin on her feet tingled somewhere between pain and pleasure before she grew used to the temperature.

'How did you find this place?' she asked Xuan.

'An older boy from the mines brought me here a couple of months ago. This is where they store our water before it gets to us.'

'Oh no, all our drinking water is going to smell of my feet.' Suong shrieked with laughter as Xuan took off his shoes and joined her. Now tired of throwing stones, the other boys joined in sloshing their feet in the dark waters while threatening to push one another in.

Suong lay back and looked at the shimmering light reflecting off the rock surface of the ceiling. She felt sleepy. The farther someone got from the air cyclers, the more oxygen levels reduced, which made a person tired, but she didn't care. This was a magical place, so fitting for a magical day, the day of the Breaker.

...

Suong and her newly found gang of friends pushed themselves into the crowd at Central Circle. Clearly, lots of people had heard about the Breaker and had the same idea. Some people had even made banners and flags.

All the shops in the Circle had closed up and pulled down their metal shutters. They must have closed up to join in the party. People were joyous and singing songs, and others were shouting out greetings to each other. Old friends and colleagues embraced and talked animatedly, catching up after years or days apart. It was like nothing Suong had ever experienced. The rush of emotions was overwhelming.

From the corner of her eye, Suong spotted the security surrounding the station. Peering through the gaps in the crowd, she studied the heavily armoured guards. Her stomach turned as the same apprehensive feeling from seeing the scabs at the union meeting shivered through her body. She tapped Xuan on the shoulder. He bent down to listen to her in the hubbub of the throng. She pointed at the security men.

'They aren't Opportunity security.'

Xuan straightened up, swaying from side to side to see through the heaving bodies. He pointed out the guards to his friends, and they all checked out the additional security. The guards wore black body armour and had balaclavas on their heads, with oxygen masks pulled up to sit on their heads like strange tiny top hats. They all had bolt guns, as well as the tasers that the Opportunity guards typically carried.

'Maybe the Breaker brings their own security?' Xuan said unsurely.

'No,' one of the shy boys said, 'they are security from Joy city.'

'How would you know that?' another boy asked dismissively.

'I get to visit my dad there every three months,' the first boy said, looking at his feet.

The Joy prison guards were renowned for their cruelty. Step out of line, and you got a bolt to the skull long before you would get put in front of a judge.

'Maybe we should get out of here?' Xuan suggested. The others all nodded in agreement and turned to make their way back out of the crowd. Just at that moment, an enormous cheer erupted as the doors of the station slid open. The crowd surged forward to glimpse the Breaker. The crowd swept Suong up immediately, her tiny frame having no hope of holding its own in the confines of the chaotic crowd.

At first, she could see Xuan trying to make his way to her, but soon she lost sight of him as the mass of bodies forced her away like a piece of driftwood in a raging river. The initial excitement and high spirits that fuelled the crowd's movements gradually changed as people started shouting and booing.

Suong could see none of what was transpiring from her vantage point. She had to work it all out from the sounds and the attitude of the surrounding strangers. Suddenly, something happened up ahead. The crowd's mood swung again, from disappointment to anger. She could hear shouts and screams and the hissing of the bolt guns ahead of her.

The tide changed direction, sweeping her away from the station. She was doing everything in her power to stay upright. She knew if she got knocked down, the stampede would crush her. It took all her skill and nimbleness to stay vertical. And then one trip and a stumble, and she was on the ground. She turned, gazing up, ready for the big work boot that would crush her skull. But as she looked up, someone looked down.

A big sinewy arm swept in and picked her up off the ground in the same way she would pick up a pencil from a desk. And somebody was clutching her tight to their body as the crowd swept them along.

'What on Mars are you doing here, little girl?' the big man asked after sucking in a deep breath. The stubble on his face scratched painfully at her forehead as they jostled along.

'I just wanted to see the Breaker,' Suong sobbed, the terrifying ordeal finally expressed as tears rolled down her face.

'Don't worry, I got you now, it will all be OK,' the big man said as the surging crowd halted and he slowed. From her higher vantage point, Suong could see they were close to the shops now. They hadn't been moving towards the exit at all. And the crowd behind was still coming. The screams and the hissing of the bolt guns were only a dozen metres behind them, and the shuttered shop windows were only metres ahead.

The crowd contracted around her as the group behind pressed harder. She felt the air sucked from her lungs as another surge hit them. But she was not the only one. An unconscious woman's face brushed against Suong's. And then, like a monster had pulled her into the depths, the woman was gone. As the crush kept tightening, the kind man's muscle-bound arms created a barrier around her. But as the seconds ticked away, she could feel him slowly weakening. The fight left him, as the air wouldn't come anymore.

'Climb!' he gasped as he lowered his hands, and with one massive effort, he ousted her body from the crowd.

Suong sucked in a deep breath as the horde spat her tiny body out like an orange pip. She was now on her hands and knees on top of the compacted press of people. One leg was stuck between two unconscious bodies. She had to stand up and push on their faces with her free foot and yank until she pulled herself free. She looked back to her saviour, but he was gone, swallowed whole in his efforts to free her.

Suong turned and ran, trying to stand on people's shoulders rather than their heads and faces, but it was an impossible task. It was like running on a shifting heap of debris. It lifted and distorted, and soon she lost any inhibition and ran on anything that would give her purchase. She could see the exit gates ahead of her. She could feel the press below her lessen as the people neared escape. Then, in a moment of carelessness, she caught her foot and fell. She slipped sideways face-first into a lamppost, the only hard object anywhere around, and then darkness.

11

The atmosphere inside the armoured truck was as intense as it had been in the Circle they had just left. Olgo eyed their security escort. While Olgo considered themself an expert reader of people, judging anything when only the eyes were visible made things that bit more difficult. Glebe and Stevie were at least outwardly composed, but Olgo knew both men well and could spot the tension in them. Tasha, however, had never been in a situation like this before. There was a tremor in her movements as she brought her hand to her face.

The doors on the side of the military truck whizzed open as they came to a halt. Their guard led them from the vehicle. Olgo looked around at their surroundings. A small tunnel, somewhat off the beaten track. Hotels were not in high demand in Opportunity City, and this one had a dingy neon sign and swing doors that looked to be hanging on by a thread. But at least they had arrived at the hotel and not the barracks or prison.

The guard captain led the way, while another four followed them in. A deserted hotel lobby greeted them. A single staff member sat behind a holo at the reception desk, but quickly hurried out on seeing their arrival and handed them each a keycard.

'I trust you will be safe here,' the guard captain snorted as their escort turned and left the building. There was a noticeable reduction in anxiety as the armoured truck drove away.

'I suggest we allow the City to calm itself before we get to work. I will see you all in the morning at breakfast,' Olgo said before heading for the stairs.

Olgo sat in the armchair in the dingy hotel room, staring at the picture screen on the wall as it scrolled through landscape images of Old Earth. Today had been a close call. Olgo considered whether Glebe and Stevie were enough security in such a chaotic city. While Micron had no military presence on the planet, they could call down marine squads based on the Micron station in orbit to beef up security. The downside to that would be the appearance of a military takeover.

Part of what had made the operation successful in Portrock City was that it had snowballed spontaneously once they had started the process. Underground unions had appeared from the shadows, and many companies had fallen in line without coercion. If they introduced the military, it might halt that organic process.

History's ability to repeat itself was astounding. Five hundred years after an industrial Earth had unionised and established workers' rights, the same thing was happening here on Mars. Except that, with outside help, the movement might gather much more momentum than was possible if left to its own devices.

The door chimed, and Olgo snapped out of their contemplations. They sent a quick text to Stevie just in case something was awry.

There was no spyhole on the door, so Olgo just pressed the button, and it opened slowly. Lisin stood outside with five security guards. He had that arrogant swagger that men in power often assume. Olgo should have seen this coming, but this planet had thrown them off their game. Lisin had removed them from the crowd and separated the team before coming for Olgo.

'Olgo, I would like to continue our discussions from last week. I think you will better understand the Guild now that you are in our city. Please come with us.'

'If you want to continue discussions, you can make an appointment, and I will see if I can fit you in,' Olgo said as they went to close the door.

Lisin put his hand on the door column, stopping the door from functioning. Olgo just stared defiantly at the Martians.

'You are coming with us, Agent, whether you like it or not.'

'I am sure I don't have to remind you, Lisin, that I am a representative of the most formidable force in this system. You will leave now, or you will pay severely for your actions,' Olgo thundered. They found it helped to turn on the drama in situations such as this one.

'I am afraid that Micron, no matter how rich it is, holds minimal sway down here. On this planet, the Guild is all-powerful, and you will not be leaving this city intact,' Lisin said with relish.

Stevie and Glebe appeared just in time, with Tasha in tow. They shouldn't have brought her. She would only complicate the situation.

'If you wanted to take me by force, you should have brought more soldiers,' Olgo said as Lisin's guards shuffled around in the hallway, nobody wanting to be on the frontline as Glebe arrived on the scene.

Despite their inferior numbers, Olgo knew that Glebe and Stevie would make mincemeat out of these guards. Stevie packed more weapons than an attack ship, and Glebe, well, Glebe would do their thing. But Lisen's arrogance didn't allow him to see the big picture. He had never dealt with an agent before. He probably didn't understand the type of people that operatives were. This underground world had blinded the man.

'I am afraid the rest of my guards are busy sorting out the mess your presence created in Central Circle. However, I have made other arrangements. Loyalty always has a price,' Lisin said, with the hint of a smile playing at the edges of his thin lips.

Shit, fuck, Stevie. Olgo turned as the devious operative whipped two pistols out of nowhere.

Olgo dodged sideways, hoping to evade the shots, but then saw the look of surprise in Stevie's eyes. Stevie was as shocked as they were at the words. Stevie's pistols swung towards the guards in the hallway.

Olgo's brain couldn't compute, but it all clicked into place as Glebe grabbed Stevie by the head and, with one massive hand, slammed their unsuspecting partner into the rock wall.

Stevie's head caved in, becoming an unrecognisable mush as his already dead body slid to the floor. Olgo raised their hands in shock as the guards turned their way.

Tasha turned to run, but one guard grabbed her before she could get far. 'Is she going to the cavern too?' the guard asked. 'No, bring her to the barracks. She may prove useful,' Lisin replied, sneering at Olgo.

Olgo ignored him while staring at Glebe, who wouldn't meet their gaze.

'Why would you do this?'

Glebe just shrugged, but Olgo swore they could see a tear welling in the silent giant's eye before feeling the taser in their back. The world blurred as the shock coursed through Olgo's body.

12

Suong woke, her head thumping and her arm bent awkwardly underneath her. She twisted her arm out, and it seemed to be OK, just numb from being lain on. Her head was a different matter altogether. Her face was tight and sore, covered in crusted drying blood. She winced as she touched a sizeable gash that decorated her forehead.

She was in transit and lying on something very irregular. She groped around her. Her fingertips found coarse material, and then she grasped a hand, but something was wrong with it. It wasn't warm like it should be. It was cold and clammy, as well as being entirely unresponsive to her touch.

Her breath caught in her throat. This must be a dream. She was lying on dead bodies. She panicked, backing away, sliding on her bum, pushing herself with her hands. One of her fingers slid into something soft and gooey. Terror froze her body as she recognised the feeling. Her finger was picking a corpse's nose. She extricated her hand slowly from the dead person's face, wiping her fingers frantically on somebody's shirt beneath her as a tremor of terror rolled through her body and a dry retch of disgust arched her neck.

Suong sat and closed her eyes, trying to slow her breathing. They must have believed her dead, covered in blood as she was, and thrown her in with the deceased. She opened her eyes and tried to focus on something, but everything was pitch black. Above her, the tunnel moved at a rapid pace. She grabbed behind her, and her hands could make out the corrugated metal side of the vehicle. She was in a mining dump truck, but going where?

Her head was woozy like the oxygen levels were low, but that could be the blow she had taken to her head. The truck was slowing now. It turned a corner, entering an enormous cavern that was lit dimly from ground level. As the vehicle backed up towards one wall, Suong could hear rough voices, but their speech was garbled.

The truck bed elevated. Suong hung to the body beneath her as they slid towards the tailgate. Ever so slowly at first, and then, as they reached 45 degrees, everything slid off in a heap, accelerating like a straight drop. Suong used all her will not to scream as the massive weight of the dead bodies rained down around her.

As quickly as it had started, the momentum of the avalanche of bodies came to a complete stop. Her whole body was in agony, but it didn't feel like any part of her had the extreme pain of something broken or twisted. Only arms and legs lay on top of her. A torso landing on her would have been the end. She opened her eyes cautiously and peered out towards the centre of the cavern through a crisscross of appendages. None of the guards seemed to pay any attention to the pile of bodies she was in. They seemed much more interested in what was happening in the centre of the cavern.

13

Glebe sat opposite Olgo in the back of the truck, massive shoulders slumped and eyes down to the floor. They were someone that was not currently delighted with their choices in life.

'How much are they paying you?' Olgo asked, which got them another dig to the ribs from the sadistic guard. But it was enough to get Glebe to look at them.

'Not about that.'

The big figure was as articulate as always.

'Then why?'

'I wanted out. Stevie wouldn't let me leave.'

'So you killed him? If you had talked to me, I could have sorted something out.'

Glebe just shrugged. Olgo couldn't understand it. Was the shy act just because they had been terrified of Stevie?

'I'm sorry I didn't pay more attention to what was going on,' Olgo said, but Glebe had retreated into themself, and no response was forthcoming.

The truck stopped, and the guards stood.

'Time to go, big fella.'

'I want to stay here,' Glebe replied.

'Job's not done till it's done.'

Glebe grumbled but climbed out of the truck, immediately wheezing with a shortness of breath. The guards wore oxygen masks, but Olgo and Glebe had nothing. Olgo flew out of the truck with a shove in the back, landing on all fours on the rough stone surface. Another boot rammed into their side, sending them spinning onto the ground, agony searing through their ribs as they tried not to spew up their lunch.

As Olgo lay prone on the ground, another truck pulled into the cavern behind them and reversed up to one wall to drop off its load before driving out again. The black-clad guards formed up in a circle around Olgo and motioned Glebe to join them. They talked to each other through comms, but their oxygen masks distorted their chatter. Olgo couldn't make any of it out.

The guards' commander pulled their oxygen mask and balaclava up over their head and looked up at Glebe. The guard had pockmarked skin, which could have been from acne or possibly from some kind of burn.

'It's time for the last part of the deal, big fella. The troopers here don't believe that you crushed that other fella's head with one hand. We want to see you do it again.' The commander grinned as they gesticulated towards Olgo. Glebe looked at the commander and shook their head.

'What do you mean, no? Either you crush their skull, or we leave you down here with 'em,' the guard said.

'Lisin said nothing about this. I done my part,' Glebe said pathetically.

'Lisin ain't here, so I am in charge, and I am giving you an order. You know how that works, don't you, Dum Dum?'

Glebe stood still. They must have realised by now that the guards had no intention of letting them live. They were just playing with Glebe, like Stevie would.

'OK,' Glebe said and slowly walked over towards Olgo. Olgo backed up on their elbows, struggling to breathe in the thin oxygen. Glebe bent down to pick Olgo up, but instead grabbed a rock the size of a football. Glebe looked at Olgo, those eyes speaking a hundred words never uttered. Olgo could see Glebe knew there was only one chance of getting out of here alive, and that was to fight. Glebe turned and threw the rock at the commander.

The rock slammed into the guard's chest, caving in their ribcage as they were flung across the cavern floor. Dead from catastrophic injury before their body came to rest. The other guards stood still, frozen in shock for a few seconds, before they charged at Glebe. Olgo would have given Glebe a fighting chance of victory under normal conditions, but with the slowing effect of the lack of oxygen, Olgo suspected this was a lost cause. However, Glebe did not know the meaning of surrender.

Some of the guards were trying to zap Glebe with their tasers. But they were designed to disable a human, not someone the size and weight of a bull. Glebe swung their giant fists like hammers at any movement. The blows were not precise or quick, but on the third attempt a guard didn't move quick enough and was crushed like an anvil had fallen on them. The attackers pulled their bolt guns but hesitated on the periphery of Glebe's reach. One brave guard ducked and swerved, shooting a bolt into Glebe's calf. But the bolt barely slowed Glebe as the heroic guard had their back broken by a falling fist.

After Glebe had pounded the fifth guard into mush, the rest decided the game was over. Someone started driving the armoured truck, and the surviving guards piled into the back as it sped off towards the tunnel entrance.

Glebe gave chase, breaking into a toddler-like run after the military vehicle. But there would be no catching them. Reaching the mouth of the cave, Glebe stopped and leaned on their knees, trying to suck in air. The truck turned the corner up ahead, and then an ear-shattering boom shook the cavern.

The tunnel exploded in a blinding flash before rocks and stones rained down. Glebe's bent-over silhouette could be seen in the dying flashes of the explosion. A mighty cracking noise split the cavern as the ceiling over the entrance separated and collapsed. Finally, Glebe had met something more substantial than they were.

14

Olgo took cover as the cloud of dust and debris from the explosion rolled over the vast cavern. They coughed and spluttered in the foul air. If the low-oxygen level was not enough, they now had to contend with the filth that filled the thin air. They covered their mouth with their shirt and sat, waiting for the dust to settle. The space occupied by trucks and a dozen guards minutes before was now an empty void of darkness. Glebe had betrayed them, but in the end, saved their life and given their own. Life was full of funny little ironies.

Olgo considered the possibilities. Their most imminent issue right now was not being able to see. The guards had stripped everything from them, even their watch. Thankfully, they had missed the emcon device. Olgo touched it, thankful for its presence. They tapped the controls, reducing the strength of the disrupter. That should give them more time until it died completely. There were probably only a few days of battery life left in it. Olgo would need to get out of here soon if they didn't want to be haunted by their distant past, never mind their current predicament.

As Olgo sat for what seemed like an age with no clue how to proceed, they could hear some slight movement somewhere behind them. It sounded too small to be a person; maybe a rat or some other vermin had adapted to this human-made subterranean world.

But then a quiet voice spoke cautiously. 'Hello.'

It was the voice of a child. Olgo considered if they could have imagined it, a side effect from the lack of oxygen? But what if their mind hadn't conjured it up?

'Are you a real person?' Olgo asked.

'Yes, I am a twelve-year-old girl,' came the child's voice again.

This definitely seemed real. What on Earth—or Mars, in this case—was a child doing down here?

'I seem to be in a bit of a predicament. But besides being lost in the dark, I am just scratched and bruised. Who are you?' Olgo asked.

'My name is Suong.'

'Nice to meet you. My name is Olgo.'

'Why are you here?' Suong asked.

'Those guards brought me down here.' The full explanation of why they were here could probably occupy a five hundred-page report.

'Was that the Breaker that was killed by the rocks up there?' the tiny voice asked concernedly. Olgo could almost hear the gears working in the child's head.

'Well, there were several Breakers, and that was one of them, but I knew them as Glebe.'

'That was the biggest person I've ever seen.'

'They were certainly not someone to be trifled with. Suong, why are you down here?'

Suong lost the cautious tone and told Olgo about the protest and a man that saved her but then died, and how she blacked out and woke up on a pile of dead bodies. Olgo just sat and listened.

'Don't worry, Suong. We will get out of here together,' they said in their best approximation of a kind voice. And then, just like that, the child was hugging them, her cheek pressed against their shoulder.

Olgo just patted her back awkwardly, not really knowing what to do with a child, or with any human contact, for that matter.

When Suong had composed herself, she sat on the ground beside Olgo.

'I am at a bit of a loss about what to do next,' Olgo said. 'Do you have any form of a torch on you?'

'I have my watch,' she said, tapping the surface, the backlight giving off a faint glow as Olgo made out the outline of her blood-covered face. It was a cheap screen watch with no holo.

'That may not get us that far,' Olgo said, resigned.

'Well, there is somewhere we could get torches,' Suong said, the last words turning into a squeak.

'Do tell.'

'Half the dead bodies in that pile are probably miners on their way home from work. They will have helmets with torches in their bags, and maybe even lanterns and halers. But I can't…' Suong trailed off.

'Don't worry. You just bring me over there, and I will get the supplies. I am sure they would be glad to help us if they were alive, and they have no use for it now,' Olgo said, realising that the child might be of more use if they could keep her from freaking out.

'Suppose you're right,' Suong said as she stood and took Olgo by the hand. Olgo stood and followed. 'Mind the lip, and be careful of the rock on your right,' she said as they made slow, steady progress across the cavern.

'Are you able to see, Suong?' Olgo asked, somewhat surprised at her ease in navigating the rough cavern floor.

'Not see, really. We call it black vision. When you are close enough to an object, you can sense it because there is less air there or something. It's hard to explain. But most people that grow up in tunnels have it.' Suong stopped. 'The bodies are a couple of metres ahead. Look for backpacks. Maybe bring them back here, and I'll sort out what we need.'

She sat facing away from the bodies as Olgo struggled the last metre before kicking an appendage and getting down on all fours to feel around.

After a couple of minutes of scrabbling about and pulling on coats and hoodies, Olgo located a backpack. They tried in vain to twist the body to remove the pack before realising how stupid they were being and loosened the buckles on the straps to pull the bag free. A beaten-up body and oxygen-starved brain didn't lead to smart decisions. Once they had found the trick, they managed to pull a number of other packs free.

As Olgo stood with their pile of scavenged loot, they realised they did not know which direction they were facing. The total darkness was all-enveloping, making them question if sight existed at all.

'Suong, I got some. Shout out so I can find the way back,' Olgo said, their voice echoing around the dank cavern.

'Over here,' Suong replied as she tapped her watch and held it over her head. Olgo made the return journey on their hands and knees, just to be safe.

They could hear Suong rooting through the pack. 'Aha,' she said as she turned on a blinding light. As Olgo's eyes adjusted to the sudden brightness, Suong turned the source of the light, a hard hat, and placed it on Olgo's head. Olgo looked down at the little girl with her face lit up properly for the first time. She wore her dark hair tied back into a ponytail, and wide inquisitive eyes peered out from under a large gash on her forehead. She rooted around in the bag and came out with a small plastic tube.

'There is a haler here as well.' She smiled up at Olgo as she handed them the tube. The child had resilience, even trapped deep below the city in a cave full of dead bodies and a stranger. Children had to be tough in this place, they concluded.

Olgo looked down at the plastic tube. 'What is this, Suong?'

'The miners use them for when they are deep down in low oxygen. Suck on this end. It opens up your lungs,' Suong said, explaining as if Olgo was a dimwit.

Olgo sucked on the plastic device and immediately felt better. They sat down and handed the tube back to Suong. She took a puff of the haler, and her face relaxed a little with the sensation.

She looked back up at Olgo. 'Better keep looking for supplies. We could be fifty miles from the city. We will need to take everything we can carry if we want to make it back.'

'First things first,' Olgo said. 'One must always put on a good appearance, especially in the worst situations.' They pulled out a bottle of water from the bag and wet an old piece of shirt, proceeding to wipe the crusty blood from Suong's face. The reduced emcon was already having an effect, but instead of fear, Olgo felt hope. A while ago they had been facing certain death. Now it was only probable.

15

A stand-alone lantern sat between them, casting massive shadows on the walls of the cavern as they sorted through what might be valuable to bring on their trip. They had packed what they could fit into two backpacks. Olgo zipped up the holdall. The items that didn't make the cut were scattered around them.

'Shall we make a start?' Olgo asked.

Suong looked at her watch. 'It's 2300. Should we not wait until morning?'

It surprised Olgo that time existed in the cavern at all.

'Maybe we should try to get out of this cave first and then have a rest?' Olgo said, glancing toward the bodies.

'Sure,' Suong said as she bounced up and started towards the collapsed entrance.

The pair stopped in front of the disordered pile of rubble. Blood was pooling at its base, but no oversized appendages were visible.

'It's completely blocked. We will have to find another way,' said Suong as she closed her eyes and leaned forward on her toes.

'Are you sure?'

'Yeah, can't you feel it? There is no air movement here at all. Tunnels always have air movement. The depth and temperature changes create winds, just like on the surface.' Suong looked sceptically at Olgo like they were some kind of imbecile.

'Can we move it?'

Suong screwed her face up. 'Not unless you have a rock breaker in your back pocket?'

'I don't even know what that is, dear. Any other ideas?'

'I can feel air coming in here from somewhere. The miners send out caterpillars—erm, they are small exploration diggers that locate ore in a promising area. They are like worms that burrow through the rock. When they locate the load, the miners then dig the main access shaft. There should be at least one small tunnel coming into the cavern. I just hope it didn't come in from above,' Suong said, looking up at the barely visible rock ceiling twenty metres overhead.

Suong moved right along one of the cavern walls, inspecting up and down the rock face with the torch on her helmet. Olgo followed suit, staying farther out to inspect higher up. It turned out to be an arduous task. The rock face was uneven and created shadows that could look like small tunnels. Suong dismissed these tricks of the light quickly after Olgo pointed them out.

They were halfway around when Olgo spotted a dark shadow up above. 'What about this one?'

The little girl walked out to them and inspected where Olgo was pointing. 'That is a tunnel, all right,' she said, studying the rock face below the potential escape route. It was about three metres above them, which didn't seem like much, but the rock face leading up to it was completely smooth.

'There are some holds higher up. You could probably whoosh me up to reach them, but there is no way you would get to them. Are you any good at climbing?' Suong asked.

'I don't know... I've never tried.'

Suong looked up at Olgo, eyes wide in disbelief. 'OK, let's keep looking. There may be another tunnel,' Suong said as she took a wide berth around the bodies. Olgo stayed and inspected the wall behind the pile. They both made their way back to the caved-in entrance with no further luck locating an alternative escape route.

Olgo twisted and stretched their neck painfully. The bruises from the beating the guards had given them hurt as the adrenaline wore off and their body temperature dropped. Suong picked up one bag and offered Olgo a drink. They took a sip; it tasted unsurprisingly like dirty rocks.

'If I can get you up to the tunnel, could we make a rope from some backpacks that I could climb up?' Olgo suggested. Suong puckered her lips and shook her head.

'There will be nothing to tie it to up there, and I couldn't support your weight.'

'Then you make the journey and bring help back here?'

Suong thought about it before shaking her head again. 'It could be days of walking to get back, and when I do, people might not believe me, and even if they did, they might not want to take the risk of rescuing you. We are in this together, and we need to keep it that way.' Suong looked down at the rock floor and breathed deeply. Eventually, she looked back up at Olgo with tears in her eyes. 'There is a way we could both get to that tunnel. A ramp. Normally you could build one with gravel, if you had an earthmover.'

'But we don't have either,' Olgo said, confused.

'No, but we have bodies.' She left the last word hanging in the air.

Olgo nodded, looking at the child's quivering lips. Olgo decided that a distraction might help the situation.

'Once you are old enough, Suong, I will have a job for you. You would make a very useful operative. How does that sound?'

'Would it be away from Mars?' she asked.

'Any posting you like.' Olgo smiled back at her, pulling Suong from her trance.

'I want to travel to the Cold on a spaceship.'

'Well, maybe keep your options open. First, we need to get out of here. You stay here, and I will start, eh, making the platform.'

'It will need to be at least a metre or so high to get a grip,' she said.

Olgo left Suong to her dreams of space travel mixed with nightmares of dead bodies while they made their way to the pile of bodies. They tapped the emcon back up to normal disruption levels. This wasn't the time to scrimp on battery power. They lugged the bodies the five metres to the tunnel entrance. Soon the sweat was dripping from Olgo's bald head. Every muscle in their body ached as they dragged the bodies one by one and stacked them under the tunnel.

At first, Olgo had randomly selected the nearest body to them, but as fatigue set in, they began searching for children or emaciated adults that were the lightest to drag. They left the children to the side, as they would be the easiest to lift on top. Olgo had witnessed and been part of some horrific incidents in their life. But they couldn't think of anything so gruesome as their current task. Every so often, their hand would move instinctively to tap behind their ear and boost the device, but each time they stopped themself. Every boost would waste more battery. They needed it to last as long as possible.

Olgo thought back to the decisions that had landed them in this situation. They had been arrogant in their approach to the Guild. Perhaps they were not as logical as they once had been. Had they changed? Or was it this job? The promotion? This planet? Something had stirred an alteration in them. But then, how could their experiences not have altered them? Playing Corpse Tetris in the depths of the Martian underworld would surely leave a mark, brainwave disrupter or no.

After what seemed like the entire night but was likely only a couple of hours, Olgo felt the pile was big enough to reach the ledge of the tunnel. They made their way back over to Suong and found her curled into a ball, gently sobbing into a backpack she was using as a pillow, with some old plastic sheeting pulled over her. Olgo lay beside the child and wrapped an arm around her. Suong grasped tightly onto their forearm and laid her head on their hand. It seemed to soothe the child, and she soon drifted off to a fitful sleep. Despite the freezing air and the rough stone mattress, Olgo's eyes blinked heavily before being dragged shut into a deep slumber.

16

Olgo led Suong to the corpse ramp. An ominous feeling surrounded them as they prepared themself to use the pile of bodies to escape. A ladder built of the flesh and bones of Suong's friends and fellow citizens.

The little girl kept her face and torch pointing high on the cavern wall. Olgo stooped and picked her up so that she wouldn't have to step directly on her friends. She seemed impossibly light compared to the bodies they had shifted during the night.

They held her in one arm, extending the other for balance as they scrambled up the precarious pile. Olgo placed their free hand against the rock surface and then elevated Suong up onto their shoulders, where she got a hold of a ledge and scurried up into the tunnel with no apparent effort at all.

Olgo threw the bags up and grabbed hold of the same ledge at full stretch. They tried to pull themself up with their arms, but no amount of effort would give them any more elevation. Olgo searched for any crevices that their feet could gain purchase on, but to no avail.

'I see what you mean about not knowing how to climb,' came Suong's voice from above.

'Not very helpful, young lady. Just give me a minute,' Olgo said as they leaned down and pulled a leg from the pile. Rigor mortis had well and truly set in at this stage. Olgo twisted the leg, wincing at the small cracking noises created as they shoved the appendage at an angle it was never meant to go. They wedged the leg's shoe against the rock wall, giving them another thirty centimetres of elevation. Olgo grabbed the ledge, put their weight on the shoe, and shoved themself up enough to get their stomach wedged on the tunnel's edge. Halfway there.

Olgo could feel tiny hands trying to get a grip on them as they squirmed around, attempting to get some purchase to pull themself all the way up. On the third attempt, Olgo wedged a knee on the ledge and started dragging themself into the passageway centimetre by centimetre as Suong pulled on their collar like a tiny anchor on a tug-of-war team.

Olgo collapsed onto the base of the tunnel and lay there, shaking from the exertion of the climb. They looked up, wheezing, as Suong handed them a haler to suck on. It was ludicrous how useless they were out of their regular environment. How was this so difficult given the reduced gravity of Mars?

Eventually, Olgo rose to their knees. 'Lead the way, young lady.'

Olgo's hands and knees grew sore and blistered from the rough stone surface as they made their way along the shaft. Suong could walk in a crouched position, but Olgo had no other choice but to travel on all fours.

'How much farther do you think we have to go?' asked Olgo.

'No way to know for sure. It could be another fifty metres or another five hundred.' Suong turned around to look at Olgo, studying the situation. 'Lie down for one minute.'

Olgo did as they were told, and Suong scurried over them and ran back down the tunnel the way they had come.

Fifteen minutes later, she was back with a pair of work gloves. Suong handed them over, breathing deeply, but her voice caught in her throat as she tried to speak.

Olgo needed a distraction. 'You could climb that wall on your own? How did you manage that?' Olgo asked, exaggerating the disbelief in their voice.

Suong looked up at them, hands shaking. But then she shook her head clear. 'I'm an excellent climber. I probably could have climbed it from the floor, but you Earthers are pretty useless underground.' She turned and continued through the shaft at Olgo's crawling pace.

Olgo had no idea how their muscles kept working through the journey. Every part of their body was screaming in agony as the tunnel continued seemingly forever. The torchlight reflection on the shiny damp rock floor in front of them became like strobe lights as their arms trembled and a headache shot pain from the base of their neck into their blinking eyes.

Suong suddenly disappeared. Olgo's heart caught in their mouth as they thought Suong had fallen into an abyss, but then she popped her head up over the lip of the tunnel.

'We have reached a main road.' Suong looked back at Olgo, a small amount of hope showing in her triumphant grin. Olgo gratefully crawled out of the tunnel and collapsed on the floor. They removed the bag from their back and lay in the foetal position on the ground.

'I'll need to rest awhile,' Olgo mumbled as they drifted off to sleep or, more likely, some kind of pain-induced coma. Suong sat by their side with her arm around them.

...

After a couple of hours, Olgo groaned awake. They never customarily dreamt. But now images of dead bodies and shrinking cavern walls that slowly closed in and crushed the two of them to death haunted their sleep. The emcon device was still functioning, albeit at a lower capacity. But they were being overwhelmed by a combination of hunger, cold, and the lack of oxygen.

Their neck and back were stiff and sore from sleeping on the cold stone surface. The blisters and welts on their hands burnt with pain, only outdone by the cuts and bruises on their knees. But at least the lancing headache had subsided.

'You ready to go?' Suong asked.

Olgo got up and stretched. It appeared impossible to do so in any way that didn't result in severe pain. A chill had set in on the cold ground, and they wanted to get moving as soon as possible.

'Which way, Suong?'

'What do you think?'

Olgo closed their eyes and turned to the right and then to the left. They could feel the tiniest of breezes from the left.

'That way?' Olgo pointed while looking at Suong for confirmation.

'We will make a Martian out of you yet,' she said as she started walking down the shaft.

If Olgo had had the energy, they would have skipped after her. Walking was so much better than crawling!

17

Olgo and Suong had walked for half a day before restlessly sleeping for a couple of hours. They had now walked another eight hours since that fitful sleep. Olgo's initial delight at being off all fours and up on their feet soon wore off as the tedium of the journey set in and the balls of their feet ached and burned.

A faint smell of dirty smoke became apparent in the tunnel. Suong motioned for them to slow and took the lead, sneaking along the tunnel edge. She looked around a corner and up ahead could see orange light dancing down the roughly hewn walls. Olgo eagerly walked past the child, keen to get back to any form of civilisation. Suong grabbed them by the hand and pulled them in towards the wall.

'Do you think the security teams will check the tunnels?' Olgo asked.

'Not out here. We aren't anywhere near the City. Must be Shadows up ahead,' Suong said, her voice quivering.

'What do you mean, Shadows?'

'They are groups of people. Well, they used to be people, usually the homeless or unemployed, who just started wandering the abandoned shafts. Some of them were mad to start with, but the low oxygen levels send them totally crazy. They live off rats and God knows what else. They are feral, like wild animals.'

Suong snuck up to the next bend in the tunnel and peered around. Olgo followed cautiously and could make out movement a hundred metres ahead. There must have been four or five Shadows. They could see now how apt the name was as their profiles danced on the walls in the flickering light.

The crooked creatures gathered around a trash fire burning in a barrel. Thick, putrid smoke bellowed up from orange and yellow slow-licking flames. The smoke crept down the passage towards them, rolling along the ceiling as it dissipated.

'Can we go around?' Olgo whispered to Suong.

'I don't think so. This is the main passage. We could try some of the smaller passages along the way, but it would be impossible to tell where they would bring us. Best off waiting until they fall asleep and then sneak by them,' she said.

'Right you are, boss. You get some rest, and I'll take the first watch,' Olgo said.

Suong's pace had been waning the last couple of hours, and no matter how much pain Olgo was in and how exhausted they were, they had to remember this resourceful girl was still just a child.

Soon Suong's breathing changed to a slow repetition that Olgo now knew as her sleeping. It was a recognition that had become normal in such a brief space of time. Olgo sat with their back to the icy wall, maintaining a watch on the Shadows in the shaft ahead as they struggled to keep their body from dozing off. The welcoming arms of sleep were so tempting. Olgo snapped out of nodding off, widening their eyes and stretching their jaw to keep the sleep at bay.

...

Olgo jolted awake. They must have dozed off. The sickening smell of dirty smoke augmented the now-familiar absolute darkness. They tried to sit up, but their hands were stuck painfully behind them. Olgo recognised the darkness was not absolute. Some light was visible, as if through a hazy weave in front of them. The realisation dawned. Olgo's arms were bound behind their back, and a dirty cloth bag was over their head.

How had this happened without them knowing? Maybe the combination of fumes and low oxygen had caused them to black out? Things were not looking good.

After a few moments, two pairs of bony hands lifted them to their feet. They removed the bag, revealing a pair of grotesque faces staring back. The creature's skin was a translucent blue under the dirt, like a stained glass window. Sweat glistened in dirty droplets on their foreheads, despite the chill in the tunnel. Rotting breath wheezed through their slack-jawed mouths as they stared at Olgo with dilated milky eyes.

Olgo looked around, searching for a sign of Suong, but they could not locate her anywhere. Maybe she had escaped these foul creatures. Olgo could only hope she would fetch help.

One creature prodded Olgo's stomach with a skeletal finger.

'Plenty a mea' on this one,' one of them said as the other nodded agreement, drool dripping from their twisted lips.

'We take dem home and feed all with dem,' came a more commanding voice from a Shadow who was busy packing up their camp farther along the tunnel.

'Can we not 'ave some now?' the drooling creature responded.

'You wanna carry dem back to the home, or you wanna let dem walk?' the voice from the tunnel reprimanded the greedy Shadow. The creature grunted and pointed up the tunnel, pushing Olgo in front of them.

Once again, Olgo thought about how lucky they were that their emotional control device was intact and functioning. While they had been experiencing some unusual feelings of late, they could still control them when they needed to. Most people would have drowned in fear and disgust right now, being held captive by lunatic cave people who were planning to eat them.

For Olgo, death was death. It was unwanted, but how it occurred was inconsequential. Olgo did have a nagging feeling about Suong, wondering where she was and if she was OK. Even with the most stoic of people, children could have a strange effect.

Olgo reflected on the conversation they'd had with Genevieve before she sent them to Mars. If this was a mission from God, now would be a good time for a miraculous intervention. Unfortunately, they had more chance of getting sunburned down here than they had of being rescued by a mythical deity.

...

Without Suong and her watch, it was tough to gauge time in the tunnels. To Olgo, it felt like they had been stumbling along for a full day, but maybe it was just half of that, or perhaps it had only been an hour. There was no way to tell, and the endless monotony of their current predicament was maddening, even for Olgo.

After a couple of attempts, Olgo outpaced their guard and caught up with the group leader.

'Where are you taking me?' Olgo asked raspingly, struggling for breath.

The leader didn't respond, they just eyed Olgo suspiciously. The leader's skin was less blue than the others, and the wildness of the eyes wasn't there. Olgo guessed this person had not been down here as long as the others and still had some of their faculties about them.

'Why did you take me captive? Maybe I am here to join you,' Olgo said, trying to sound reasonable despite their trouble breathing.

'You're not one of us,' the leader replied simply.

'I could be… I could help your people.'

'You are one of them, not a worker. Too much fat on your bones. Your people put us down here!' the leader stated, anger creeping into their voice.

'I mightn't be one of you, but I believe we're on the same side. I came here to help the people of Mars. But the Guild captured me and dumped me down here. Help me, and I can help you,' Olgo said imploringly.

'Richer's lies,' the leader shouted while shoving Olgo in the chest. Olgo tripped over their own feet and landed in a wheezing bundle on the stone floor. Some of the other Shadows tittered as someone kicked Olgo to get up and continue on.

After another indeterminate amount of time, the leader signalled, and the group formed a camp of sorts. One of them lit up the dirty stove as another produced a cooking pot and some stinking ingredients. Olgo's guard shoved them to the floor and thrust the dirty bag over their head again. Soon, the nauseating smoke was tainted with the smell of a foul broth. Olgo's stomach rumbled with hunger while their body physically gagged at the thought of eating something so disgusting. Luckily, Olgo didn't have to decide whether to try the broth or not.

Soon the captors' rasping wheezes turned to snores as they dozed off one by one. Olgo tried to hear if all four Shadows were sleeping or if one was still awake, keeping guard. But it was impossible to differentiate the snores.

With the emcon running on minimum, Olgo had expected the trauma from their youth to come tumbling back. The experiment that had left them scarred for life. Olgo's parents had thought they were doing a great thing for their child. Implanting memories from Dr Statler, a deceased scientific genius, should have made Olgo a child prodigy. But what nobody stopped to consider was that you can't separate memories. Nobody knew about the type of things Statler liked to do for fun, who Statler had chained up in his basement, and what that could do to a child's mind. But right now, none of the horror was seeping in. All Olgo could think about was Suong. How strange.

...

A hand shook Olgo awake. A tiny hand. The bag was pulled from their head but to no avail, as everything was in total darkness. A wave of relief swept over them as a small finger pressed against their lips, and Olgo nodded. A hand guided Olgo onto their stomach and then started cutting at Olgo's bonds. Soon they felt the strapping give way and enormous relief at being able to move their arms once more.

'Grab my foot and crawl after me,' Suong's tiny voice, barely audible, whispered into Olgo's ear. Olgo got up on all fours and started a journey on bare hands and knees for the second time since being dumped into the depths of Mars.

This time, the journey was in absolute darkness, so they moved even slower than before. Olgo held Suong's right foot in their hand and moved it every time the child crawled forward. The pace was unbelievably tedious, the raw burst blisters on Olgo's hands and knees searing with pain, but Olgo didn't care. They were back together. The gasping snores of the Shadows faded slowly as they inched away from the makeshift camp.

After turning the first corner in the tunnel, Suong stopped and sat back against the wall. Olgo felt the pile of their bags. The child had been busy.

'I have left my watch in the opposite tunnel. The alarm should go off soon, flashing and bleeping. Once they move towards it, we need to run,' Suong whispered into Olgo's ear.

Olgo reached out, feeling through the dark for the child, taking her in their arms and holding her in a tight embrace. Tears welled inexplicably in Olgo's eyes for the first time that they could remember. Just then, a commotion kicked off in the tunnel behind them.

'Quickly,' Suong said as she turned on a torch. They donned their backpacks, and Olgo fell in behind her as they broke into a laboured jog.

18

After what seemed like an eternity, Suong stopped and motioned for Olgo to be silent. She listened intently.

'I can't hear anything behind us and we are getting close to the City now. You can feel the oxygen. We should be safe from here. Shadows get shot on sight if they come back into the City.' Suong turned and walked on.

'Maybe I should find some sort of disguise in case we run into security?' Olgo said, kicking through some piles of rubbish at the edge of the tunnel.

Suong laughed at the ridiculousness of her new friend. 'You think you still look like an Earther?'

'I guess not,' Olgo said, looking down at their torn and grubby clothes.

Suong led them through the City, back towards the pit. She was so happy to be almost home. Olgo had turned out to be a very good person, and a good friend. But she needed her mother, the strongest person she knew. Her mother would make everything better. She would even help Olgo escape from the City.

But as they approached the lift to the pit, the relief and thankfulness that Suong was feeling started to wane. Something was wrong. Someone had shoddily tied warning tape around the lift entrance. The cage itself was not there, and nothing showed up on the digital readout about when it would arrive.

Suong turned to a passing elderly woman in the tunnel.

'What is the matter with the pit cage?' she asked.

The old woman stopped and looked at her through narrow eyes. 'Where you been hiding, child? Don't you know nothing?'

'We are just back from a week's work shift down the deep mines. What happened?'

Seemingly satisfied with Suong's explanation, the woman replied, 'Security said the pit council was who planned the riot. So they dropped a bomb down there, and the pit went bang!'

'With everyone in it?' Suong asked, disbelief in her voice.

'Far as I know. You were lucky you were away,' said the woman as she turned and continued on her way. Suong stood frozen on the spot, unable to process the information. Olgo put a hand on her shoulder and squeezed gently. This couldn't be true.

'They couldn't just kill a whole village like that, could they?' she asked Olgo.

'I don't know what happened here, but I promise you I will find out, and those who perpetrated this crime will pay,' Olgo said, venom dripping in their voice.

Olgo squatted down to Suong's height and held her at arm's length.

'It's probably not safe here. Is there anywhere else we can go?'

Suong shook her head and sniffled, wiping her nose with a dirty sleeve. There was nothing left. Everyone who meant anything to her was dead.

'Let's just start walking,' Olgo said. 'We are too obvious standing here by the emergency tape.' Olgo took her by the hand and slowly led her down the tunnel towards the city centre.

Once they were in a busier thoroughfare, Olgo directed them to the tunnel side and sat down on a rock ledge.

'I know you can't process this now, and I am so sorry to be blunt with you, but I need you to listen. This is important. We need to get to Portrock City. I have people there that will look after us. We will have to get on the train somehow.'

How could Olgo expect anything from her now? But then they had to do something, and Olgo had no idea how Mars worked. Earthers were so naïve.

'The overground trains cost a fortune, and only employers can buy tickets. Even if we had credit, they wouldn't allow us to buy tickets.'

'Let's have a look around the station and see if there is any way to sneak on,' Olgo said. Suong just shrugged.

They entered Central Circle. Work crews were repairing shop fronts, the carnage from the week before slowly being erased. Suong stared vehemently at a pair of security guards walking by, trying to bore holes in their heads with her eyes. She could see Olgo dipping their head in the opposite direction, but the guards didn't even glance at the filthy duo as they continued on their patrol.

Olgo seated them on a bench with a view of the station entrance. There was only one way onto the train, and they had beefed up security in and around the Circle. Olgo spent an hour watching the station. Suong slumped against them, snivelling. She kept imagining ways that her family could have survived, before dismissing them as childish fantasies.

17

Olgo sat in Central Circle, watching the coming and going of the security at the train station with Suong in a heap at their side. Out of nowhere, the emcon device bleeped behind Olgo's ear and the battery died, shutting off the waves completely for the first time in twenty years.

Olgo waited for the images to resurface, surely now blended with the horrors of the past few days. Olgo held their breath, ready for the tidal wave to overwhelm them. But it never came. They looked down at the heartbroken child, and the only thing that crept through from their unbridled psyche was an overpowering desire to protect and care for Suong.

Olgo put their arm around Suong and held her head tight against their chest, rocking her ever so slightly.

'You have lost everything, Suong. But I promise you I will do everything I can to care for you,' Olgo whispered into the child's ear. They had no way of knowing if the words even registered with the girl. But for now, words were all they had.

Olgo looked up as a disabled child hobbled towards them on a crutch. The child stared at them through a single eye, the other covered in a patch above a broken cheekbone.

'I have no credits to give, I am afraid,' Olgo said, trying to get rid of the beggar.

The child continued to stare at them.

'Suong?' the child said.

Suong slowly drew her face from Olgo's chest and looked towards the disabled child.

After a moment's pause, she replied. 'Xuan?'

The child smiled a crooked, painful smile through the stitches on their cheek.

Suong stood up and embraced Xuan, who stared suspiciously over Suong's shoulder at Olgo.

'Who is that?' Xuan asked.

'This is Olgo,' Suong said, dragging Xuan over towards the bench. 'Olgo rescued me from the depths.'

'Since when did you need rescuing?' Xuan asked astutely.

'You are right, of course. Suong rescued me from the depths. But right now, we have nowhere to go. Do you know of somewhere we can shelter?'

Xuan looked at Olgo, analysing what Suong had said. Olgo's Earther accent must be obvious, regardless of their dishevelled looks.

'I have found no one else alive from the pit, but the union has been looking after me. And I know that someone there will be pleased to see you, Suong. Follow me.'

...

Olgo sat a couple of hundred metres from the entrance to Newstar Clothing. Suong and Xuan waited by the door. A slender young lady left the factory entrance. At first, the woman tried to avoid Suong as the child approached her. But after a moment, the recognition dawned on her. She knelt down on one knee and embraced Suong. That was a good sign. Olgo watched as Suong wept and Xuan explained things to the woman, before pointing down the tunnel towards Olgo.

Olgo stood up as the three Martians approached. Suong's boss couldn't have been more than twenty years old. On Earth, she would still be a student. Here on Mars, she ran a factory crew. She had straight black hair pulled back into a tight ponytail and wore makeup to soften her face's strong angles.

'Boupha, this is my friend Olgo. They saved me in the caverns.'

Olgo smiled and extended a filthy, blistered hand. Boupha took the hand and shook it, all the time scrutinising Olgo through narrowed eyes.

'You are a stranger to me, Olgo, but Suong here says you are a friend, and she is a smart girl, so I believe her. I haven't space in my family home for all three of you. But I can take Suong, and I will talk to some friends about taking you in for a couple of days.'

'Thank you, Boupha. I sincerely appreciate your help,' Olgo said.

'You're an Earther?' Boupha asked.

'Yes,' Olgo nodded. The best subterfuge was always the simplest. Always give as little information as possible. Usually, people made up their own presumptions that were much more believable than anything Olgo might tell them.

'And you arrived here from Portrock City the day of the riot?' Boupha asked, like she already knew the answer.

Olgo nodded. This girl was smart. Usually, that wouldn't be a problem for Olgo, but the exhaustion, the pain and the lack of their emcon device meant they would not do well in an interrogation right now.

'Are you one of the Breaker's entourage?' Boupha asked, staring at Olgo's eyes, looking for the lie. Olgo looked back, weighing up their options. Could they trust this girl? What choice did they have?

'Yes, I was travelling with the Breaker's. But as you can see, I am the one that has been broken since then.'

'I have to say, you don't look like the Breaker from the stories,' Boupha said, a slight smile hinting at the corner of her thin lips. 'Come, I have someone who I think would like to meet you.' She turned and took Suong by the hand, leading the group down the tunnel.

Olgo just hoped Boupha wasn't bringing them to a security station. It was pretty jading having people try to kill you all the time.

20

Olgo had been lodging with one of Boupha's friends for a week. They couldn't believe how much the few days in the tunnels had taken out of them. They had slept for two full days after arriving. Since then, they had slowly gotten their strength back, but Olgo suspected that physically their body might never fully recover. As for their mental state, they couldn't even begin to pick at that minefield. So far, Olgo had showed no signs of a breakdown since the emcon device had died. Not that they'd had to deal with any life-or-death situations since then. But that day would come soon enough.

Their host, Bolo, was an interesting character. He owned and lived in a small garage which specialised in fixing small-scale mining equipment. He was in his fifties and had a small, wiry frame that was deceptively strong for his muscle mass. His head was bald naturally, and his face was cragged and veined from years of drinking Martian moonshine, but his eyes and brain were still sharp and active—at least when he was sober.

He marched around his workshop with purpose, always busy, flying through the work that needed to be done so he could clock off as early as possible for that first sip of the drink. During his work time, Olgo had some engaging and thought-provoking conversations with the man. However, after a few drinks, the stories got wilder and more pompous.

'There isn't a single workshop in this city that is running as it should.' Bolo said. 'How could I work somewhere that doesn't train people proper, or that doesn't use the proper safety gear? That's why I never settled in a big company. But old Benji gave me a job here and let me run the place. When he died, he left it all to me. He had a few nephews that weren't happy about that, but I ran the bastards. Big bastards, they were too.'

Bolo was only a couple of sips into the glass of moonshine. In an hour's time, the nephews would be gigantic killers in makeshift mech suits. But Olgo had gotten smart and intended to be tucked up in bed by that time.

'Of course, back in those days, there was never even mention of a union,' Bolo continued. 'But once the underground union formed, I decided that, even though I wasn't a worker, they could do with my help. Being a business owner means I don't need permission to travel between the cities. So I started out as the go-between for any of the big moves. All top-secret, of course. If I told you, I would have to kill you. Well, between you and me, this one day, they sent me to Portrock to deliver…'

Olgo zoned out. They had heard this one before and had also managed not to be killed afterwards. They wondered if it was worth sticking it out to see how fantastical the ending would be today.

Olgo was nervous about the imminent escape to Portrock. Bolo was fixing up an ancient surface scout vehicle. The machine used a combustion engine and could carry extra fuel to make the long trip to Portrock City. Bolo had explained the different things that could go wrong with the vehicle and how to repair them, but Olgo understood very little. This machine was a long way from Olgo's personal drone back on Earth.

The other major issue with the vehicle was that it had no cab, meaning that Olgo would have to wear a suit for the entire trip and carry a stack of oxygen tanks to sustain them on the journey. Boupha had turned out to be extremely smart and helpful. She estimated the trip would take about five days in the motor vehicle. She had plotted the route to avoid the rail line and any other overground structures between the two cities.

'When you make it to Portrock, call into that stingy old beggar and tell him not to forget the credit he owes me. So anyway…' Olgo nodded, pretending to be fascinated by Bolo's story.

Olgo feared the overground trip to Portrock would be an impossible feat, but they could discover no other way. Without their watch and the access codes within it, they couldn't get a message outside of this city. Well, at least not one that anybody would believe was from Olgo.

The communication laws on Mars were draconian, and since the Breaker had arrived in Opportunity, the city's authorities had disabled all social media and long-range comms completely.

Bolo started into a story about flipping a mining cart when drunk and spending the night sleeping in ignorance, not realising he was hanging over the edge of an abyss. It was one of Bolo's more entertaining stories, but Olgo's mind drifted back to Suong and the journey they had been through. Olgo had formed a bond with the child, an emotional bond far more substantial than Olgo had thought possible. Every day, Suong would pop in to visit Olgo on her way home from work.

The little girl lifted Olgo's mood. Every day they found themself tapping the floor and watching the clock in anticipation of Suong's visit. They no longer feared the emotions that bubbled below the surface. Far stronger positive emotions had supplanted the bad ones. Olgo knew it was stupid, but the scariest thing about the overground trip to Portrock City wasn't the days in a vac suit or the risk of their life. The worst thing was going to be how they could bear to leave Suong behind.

Bolo believed they would have everything ready for the journey in another two days, and Olgo was contemplating how they could prolong that even a little longer.

Up to this point in their adult life, reason governed every decision Olgo made. It was what made them who they were. Now, these strange feelings and emotions were clouding their mind. They worried about how they could function properly again. Olgo couldn't be sure that they would. But there was no way they could go back to blocking out the emotions that they had discovered. On their second day at Bolo's, the mechanic had rigged up a charger for the emcon device. After staring at the tiny contraption for an eternity, Olgo eventually charged it but was too scared to put it back on. The fear of losing this… love, was too strong. The next day, Olgo dropped the device in a vat of cleaning fluid and that was that.

'After that night, I swore I would never drink and drive again.' Bolo finished the embellished story.

'Probably for the best.' Olgo replied. 'Anyway, it is time for bed. I have to regain my strength for the trip.'

'Right you are, boss. One for the road?' Bolo asked, eyebrows raised.

Olgo recognised the loneliness in his eyes. Drink could never fill the space of family.

'A small one now, Bolo.'

21

Suong and Boupha came to the antiquated airlock to say goodbye to Olgo. The old vac suit didn't fit Olgo very well—it was made for someone taller and skinnier—but it was the best they could find.

Olgo took Bolo by the hand.

'You are a good man, if a terrible drunk. When I get back, I will reward you handsomely!'

'Well, you better get a fuckin move on then,' Bolo said with a laugh as they walked over to the makeshift airlock controls.

Olgo turned to Boupha. 'You have gone above and beyond for me. Your kindness will not be forgotten.'

Boupha just smiled and nodded, which was a lot for the rather serious woman.

Suong jumped up and clung onto Olgo's neck as they turned to the child. Olgo embraced her back.

'I will be back, little one, I promise you. Someday I will take you to the stars.'

Olgo pulled Suong from the embrace, smiling, and put on their helmet before the tears came. They watched Suong bravely hide her tears by pretending to wipe her nose on her sleeve.

Boupha tightened the helmet-clamping mechanisms, and Olgo walked awkwardly in the ill-fitting suit into the airlock. Bolo revved a mini generator that started working the hydraulics, and the inner door began closing slowly.

The solid sheet of metal descended, separating Olgo from their friends, perhaps forever if Olgo didn't survive the wastelands. The inner door sealed, and the pressure adjusted in the airlock before the outer door shuddered and began its stop-start journey to being open.

It was night-time outside for another couple of hours. They had thought it better to leave under cover of darkness. The Phobos moon was full in the sky, but that wouldn't last long as it passed through all its phases in a single night. It was much smaller than Earth's Moon. Its irregular shape gave it an unfinished look, and its size meant it cast very little light on the planet. Olgo had a navigator strapped to the front of the vehicle to guide them on their journey. The maps of areas close to the cities were detailed enough that driving in the dark was doable, though not easy. Farther out into the desert, driving would only be possible during daylight.

Olgo turned the key and revved the scout. This was the first test to see if Bolo had successfully mixed the fuel so that it would work in the thin Martian atmosphere. So far, so good. Olgo applied pressure to the accelerator pedal, revving the combustion engine, and the vehicle moved jerkily out of the airlock doors. A small pile of sand had formed in front of the old door. The scout's big buggy wheels pulled the vehicle over it and out into the black desert.

Olgo drove cautiously along the path designated by the navigator, only occasionally deviating from the course if a rock or hollow came into view at the last second. The progress was tediously slow. Ice crystals formed inside Olgo's visor, impeding their vision and ability to work the controls. After two hours of driving, the chimney stacks and vents that were evidence of the city below thinned out. After three hours, the sun rose, and Olgo could see no more indications of the city. Olgo moved the small vehicle up through its gears as Bolo had shown them. The operation of the gears proved much more complicated than they had expected.

Soon, the rocks and gravel gave way to sand and small dunes, creating a beautiful, oceanlike landscape. The rising red sun shimmered across the faux seascape, creating the most beautiful sunrise Olgo had ever seen. They thought of the millions dwelling in the rocks below the surface who had never set eyes on the sun. What strange worlds we live in, Olgo thought as they drove through the dunes, the up and down motion dropping their stomach like a shuttle in final descent.

At that moment, emotions overwhelmed Olgo. Suong had opened up a whole new world to them. New feelings engulfed them as they breathed in the beauty of the place and the hope of what this planet could become. Despite their struggles, Olgo was elated as they drove across the uncharted Martian hinterland. Opportunity City had almost killed the old Olgo, but the kindness of a small child had given birth to something new inside of them.

...

As the sun descended on the horizon behind them, Olgo found a small rock face to set up camp below. They refilled the rover with fuel and restocked their suit with oxygen before inflating the one-person tent. Temperatures were due to plummet to under −100 degrees Celsius tonight, and Olgo's vac suit wouldn't be able to cope with those extremes for an entire night.

Olgo sat on a rock and started fiddling with the food intake attachment. Usually, someone on a prolonged journey on the surface would have a suit with liquid sustenance built-in. But this suit was only built for spending a single work shift out on the surface. After awkwardly eating some meal biscuits, Olgo reluctantly went to figure out how the waste removal apparatus that Bolo had rigged up for them worked.

They slid into the inflated tent, which was filled with insulation gas. They sealed up the entrance valve and lay in the centre of the bubble. The tent walls closed in around the suit, holding them as if in a fluid. This must be what it feels like to be in the womb. How apt, as I am born anew, Olgo thought as they drifted off to a peaceful sleep.

22

After five days of travelling over the Martian surface, Olgo was no longer enthralled by the alien planet's beauty. Their body was stinking inside the old vac suit, and the thought of proper food and an actual toilet seemed like luxuries beyond belief.

They had risen early to approach the entry point at first light. The airlock belonged to a company called Landway-Tanyui which was indirectly owned by Micron. It was a good bet this would be the safest access point into Portrock City.

Olgo travelled the last couple of hundred metres on foot so as not to raise any alarm. They waited until a vehicle exited the airlock, leaving the outer door open. Olgo entered the airlock and pressed the cycle button inside. The exterior door closed, and the air cycled through. The inner door opened up to a warehouse full of confused-looking workers.

Olgo stumbled into the loading bay, trying to remove the helmet. A couple of workers came up and helped them get it off. They all stood back in shock as the helmet disconnected and five days of body odours poured out at them.

'You OK, mate?' a friendly voice asked. 'I think you're in the wrong place.'

'I need to speak with someone in Micron,' Olgo said with urgency. The worker assessed Olgo for a moment. Here, Olgo's Earther accent worked in their favour as the worker nodded. 'OK, mate. Hey, boss, this fella needs to speak with someone in Micron. Seems like they took the long route from Earth,' the worker shouted over their shoulder.

The chief walked over to them, looking suspiciously at Olgo. 'You know who you are looking for, mate?'

'Ling in Compliance,' Olgo said.

'Give me two seconds and I'll check with them. Who will I say is looking for them?' they said as they gave Olgo a smile and a pat on the back.

'Tell them it's Agent Olgo.'

The chief's demeanour changed from friendly to reverent as they pulled up the dialler on their watch.

...

Ling sent a security detail to pick Olgo up. The guards brought a change of clothes and a portable air shower. Olgo disposed of their Vac suit in a skip outside the Landway-Tanyui loading bay. They doubted any form of cleaning could bring it back to being usable again.

Ling met Olgo at the doors to Micron HQ, along with another agent.

'I can't believe it's really you,' Ling said as he shook Olgo's dirt-ingrained hand. 'This is Agent Flint. They took over from you after the incident in Opportunity.' Ling motioned to the other agent.

'Flint in Portrock, eh? How appropriate.' Olgo smiled, immediately slipping back into their old self as the occasion required.

'Ling, we will need a private room. Flint, I will need to be brought up to date on everything that has happened since I have been gone,' Olgo said matter-of-factly as they strode through the Micron entrance.

Ling led them to a briefing room, blathering the entire way there. At least one person was happy to see Olgo. They suspected Flint wasn't that excited about their miraculous return. But Flint didn't understand. Genevieve had sent Olgo on a mission from God. And here was Olgo—risen from the dead. Ling opened the door for them and left the two agents alone.

'I will need to debrief you before we discuss anything,' Agent Flint said, eyeing the grime encrusted Olgo suspiciously.

'Of course, however, once I am debriefed and back up to speed, I will take over this operation again. I am working directly for the CEO and therefore have seniority here, agreed?' Olgo said, a new resolve and determination coursing through their body.

Agent Flint looked slightly aggrieved but nodded their head after a moment's hesitation.

'I was Genevieve's favorite once, you know, but then I fucked up. Nothing lasts long in this business,' Flint said as they popped up a small camera drone. Olgo told the story of the riot and what had happened subsequently. They recounted the story in the manner that the old Olgo would have told it, without emotion or attachment to any of the persons involved. Olgo also left out Glebe's deception and instead painted him as the hero that saved their life in the cavern.

After they had finished, Flint sat back and blew out a deep breath, the scepticism replaced by something that might possibly be described as being impressed. 'You have been through quite the ordeal. Are you sure you wouldn't rather get some grub and a proper wash before we continue?'

'One thing I have learnt recently is that the body can endure immeasurably past where you believe it can. All that can wait. Fill me in on the current situation,' Olgo replied.

Agent Flint's left eye twitched as Olgo insisted on continuing the discussion. The agent might have been impressed with Olgo's story, but they were still reluctant to give up control of the mission.

Flint took a deep breath before continuing. 'Well, despite how it ended for you and the people in Central Station, the Opportunity riots had quite the effect on the planet,' Flint said gruffly. 'The Guild put it out that protesters murdered you and your team, but footage leaked from the riots and it was clear the security guards were the aggressors, so nobody believed the spin. A wave of outrage and revolution swept the planet. No one could believe how little power the Guild had in reality. They held authority with a theatre of threats. Within a week, the underground unions had risen and overthrown Guild security. The unions formed city councils, and with our help those councils are now working on a plan to create a planetary government. But that's the good news.'

Flint engaged the tabletop holo. At first, Olgo thought the images were of the riot in Central Station which Suong had been caught up in. But then they realised it was another city and another riot. Olgo watched as protesters sabotaged machinery and looted shops. Another clip showed protesters beating someone, presumably an owner, to death.

'Some cities are in the middle of gang warfare right now. We estimate 50 billion credit's worth of damage, and that is before the disruption to supply lines has even been considered. How much better off the Martian people will be at the end of all this is to be seen. I have channelled most of our resources into supporting the unions and hoping they can take control of the situation. But it's a slow process. Most of these people have never led or had any type of control over their own destiny. Outside of all that chaos are the only two cities still in Guild control, the Joy and Opportunity.' Flint pulled up a holo map and pointed towards an atlas of the planet's cities.

Olgo sat open-mouthed, staring at the holo. They had presumed that every city was under lockdown like Opportunity. But a revolution had swept the planet organically. Olgo smothered down the unfamiliar feelings of both pride in creating a revolution and shame at the mess it had become.

'So, what is the situation with the two hold-out cities?' Olgo asked, pushing the images from the rest of the planet to the back of their mind.

'Well, there is not much we can do with the Joy. Probably not a good idea to let a bunch of maniacal prisoners form a council and run their own prison. So our current position is to leave it in Guild hands. Opportunity is another story altogether. The Guild council has barricaded themselves in. Since the riot, martial law has been in place, so we have very little info about the situation. We know that the total lockdown means people inside do not know what has been happening on the rest of the planet. The murder of the rioters and subsequent executions seem to have suppressed any uprising there.'

'So, what is the plan?'

'So far, our plan has been to wait and see. I believe martial law can only last so long,' Flint said, shrugging.

'Do we have marines nearby?' Olgo asked.

'There are two squads on board the Micron station in orbit, but I think that should be the last resort,' Flint said with a worried look.

'The Guild murdered my team, along with hundreds of innocent civilians, and dumped us all in a hole. The last resort is now. Get those marines down here. I will lead the attack in the morning,' Olgo said, standing. 'Now, I am off to eat and use an actual toilet. You have done an excellent job, Agent Flint.' Olgo patted the shocked Flint on the back before striding from the room.

23

Olgo climbed the ramp of the troop carrier. They wore a modern armoured and perfectly fitted vac suit, a million miles from what they had been wearing for the past five days. Two dozen mech suits hung from the troop carrier's walls like carcasses in a robot butcher's. Each suit was three metres of pure titanium armour, all personalised to the marine's taste. An array of weapons and mods decorated each of the terrifying machines.

The ship took off as Olgo cycled through into the atmospheric area of the craft. The Marine commander met them on the other side.

The tall woman introduced herself. 'Commander Midas, Ser.'

'A spacer in a planetary marine unit?' Olgo asked, looking up at the woman towering above them.

'Not for long, Ser. Orders came through just now. We are shipping out for the Cold. This will be our last mission Mars-side before the long haul to Neptune Station.'

'Still, an impressive feat that you can operate in real gravity. I am sure I would find it impossible if our roles were reversed.'

'This is only Mars, Ser. Gravity here is a piece of piss,' she said, grinning down at Olgo.

'Good for you. Now let's have a look through this plan of attack.'

The rest of the Marine squad gathered around as Olgo swiped the attack plan over to the central holo. It was a relief to have a watch once again. They had felt naked without one.

'Our aim today is to capture all the members of the Guild Council. I have attached their IDs. Make sure you are all on the lookout for them. We will also need to take control of the security headquarters and the train station. I expect zero casualties today. The people of this city have suffered enough death in the past month.' Olgo paused for effect.

'We will split our forces in three and enter through three airlocks in key positions simultaneously. They should not see us coming. Once we are in, we expect little resistance. There is no intel to suggest they have anything resembling a mech, so I fully intend our massive show of force to lead to a swift surrender. We should not have to fire a single shot,' Olgo said as they circled the holo.

'You really know how to take the fun out of things,' the huge Earther subcommander quipped.

Olgo turned on them. 'This is your job, Marine, not a day out. The population's safety is of the utmost importance to the CEO herself. You will carry out this mission as you are instructed! Understood?' Olgo shouted up at the big marine.

'Yes, Ser,' came the startled response.

Commander Midas took over the presentation. 'Rail gun rounds are highly dangerous in the caverns. We don't want the roof coming down on us. You will be issued with rubber bullets and taser mods. Live rounds are a last resort, for everybody's safety. This will be our last action before the long haul to the Cold. Let's keep it nice and simple. Get through this, and you can drink yourselves into oblivion for the next two years,' Midas said to nods and grunts of approval from her squad.

...

The ship shuddered at the stomp of the mechanised boots marching onto the Martian rocks, something akin to a minor earthquake.

Olgo followed the marines out, feeling like a dwarf surrounded by these vast killing machines. The marines split into three groups, and Olgo followed Commander Midas and her marines to the designated airlock.

One marine hooked up to the external controls and hacked the security system.

'Red team in position.'

'Green team in position.'

'Blue team in position,' the squad commanders reported as they secured their airlocks.

'On my mark, we are go!' came Midas's voice through the comms. The outer airlock door slid open. The eight mechs and Olgo squeezed inside.

The airlock cycled, and the inner door opened to an empty warehouse. Two mechs led the way as the rest filed out behind, with Olgo and Midas at the column's rear. Olgo hurried to keep up with the massive strides of the mechs.

They emerged from the factory onto a busy thoroughfare. The locals stared in disbelief at the mech suits, painted up in exotic colours and weaponised plumage.

'Let's get a move on, people. We don't want to let the bad guys get away,' Midas said, as the marine leader turned and headed towards the Guild's headquarters.

A loud crack originated from somewhere nearby, and Olgo found themself slammed to the ground by a big mech hand. Midas was probably treating them gently. But it certainly didn't feel like that.

'We have a dozen armed guards with powder rifles behind a shield wall, Ser,' a marine reported to Midas, who was covering Olgo with her big mech body.

'Hold your fire,' Midas ordered. 'Let's see if we can flank them and take them alive.'

'Doesn't look like we will have time for that. Sensors have another thirty bodies coming up behind them,' the marine reported.

'Shit, take cover.' Midas dragged Olgo around a rocky corner. 'I am afraid your plan for a zero-casualty mission may not be working out as planned. We can't take a position with that many people without using lethal force.'

The cracks of the old-fashioned rifles ceased suddenly, replaced by shouts and screaming.

'You might want to take a look at this, Ser,' Midas said.

Olgo peered around the rough-hewn rock corner. One of the armed security guards came flying out over the shield wall. Olgo spotted Bolo's bald head among the hubbub. The wiry mechanic was wielding a large spanner with some effect on the other side of the barrier. Word of their arrival must have spread quickly through the caverns.

'Some old friends,' Olgo said to the bemused Midas.

'I guess you don't want to mess with fellas that swing picks for a living,' Midas said, clearly impressed by the rabble that Bolo had brought together.

'Very true, although we may want to step in before they murder those guards,' Olgo replied.

Midas sent a mech to bring the situation under control while the rest of the squad proceeded to the Guildhall.

As they approached, Olgo watched two security guards make a run for it away from the entrance. Two bolt guns lay discarded on the ground. A weapon which seemed so terrifying a few weeks previous now appeared like a pea shooter abandoned in the dust.

The doors were locked, but a marine made quick work of them with a single punch. Midas left two marines on guard outside as the rest of the squad proceeded inside. Six Guild security guards stood in the foyer staring at the metal door, now bent beyond recognition on the floor. They dropped their guns and raised their hands without a word.

Olgo walked up to them. 'Where are the bosses?'

'Fourth floor,' the guard replied, pointing to the stairs. A marine led the guards outside in a chain gang. Olgo followed the remaining mechs up the grand staircase, bits of polished marble splintering and flying from the ornate steps as the giant boots crunched their way up, flight by flight.

On the fourth floor, Midas kicked open the large oak doors to the boardroom. The Guild Council members sat around the boardroom table as if nothing was going on, possibly in some vain show of defiance.

'Clear,' Midas shouted as Olgo made their way into the room. Olgo slowly removed their helmet and placed it on the table. Garcia's shock was plain to see on her face, but Lisin hid his surprise far better.

'Thank you all so much for gathering here. It makes my life so much easier,' Olgo began as they paced around the table. 'You are all under arrest on one count of conspiracy to abduct an agent and on multiple counts of murder. I don't have a figure yet for the murders, but trust me when I say that I will dig up every single body from that cavern, and all of those innocent people's names will be read out in your court case. Take them away. If they resist, feel free to slap them around a bit.' Olgo slapped the table as the mechs manhandled the council members from the room. Unfortunately, no resistance was forthcoming. Having such an overwhelming force that people just gave up easily led to a disappointing de-escalation in any attack.

'Ser, we have a situation at the security centre. We found one of your party. She is in a bad way and won't let anyone near her. Maybe seeing you would help?'

'Let's go,' Olgo said, hurrying from the room and heading back down into the street.

I could get used to having a mech escort all the time, Olgo thought to themself as people scattered before them. A familiar figure approached Olgo, and Midas moved in front of them protectively.

'Don't worry, it's another friend,' Olgo said as they moved to greet Boupha, whose mouth was hanging open in amazement.

'You managed some amount of socialising in your time here,' Midas said, shaking her giant robot-like head.

Boupha approached warily, eyeing the mechs that surrounded Olgo.

'You said you would be back, but I didn't know you had such big friends.'

'I seem to find friends everywhere I go these days,' Olgo said. 'Are you well, Boupha? Is everything OK with Suong?'

'Yes, she is at home with my parents. I wouldn't let her come, much to her annoyance.'

'I can imagine.' Olgo laughed. 'Actually, if you wouldn't mind doing me a favour, I have a situation that is not best solved by gigantic killing machines. Perhaps you could help me out?'

'Of course.' Boupha nodded as she joined Olgo's entourage on their way to the security station.

Midas escorted Boupha and Olgo into a cell at the back of the dilapidated station. Tasha sat curled up in a corner, the beautiful woman barely recognisable now. Her blouse was torn and bloody, her hair was a tangled mess, and more than half her fingers were missing.

Olgo approached her slowly. 'Tasha, it's me, Olgo,' they said as they hunkered down in front of her. The woman just glanced up and then back down again. A wave of revulsion swept through Olgo's body as those beautiful brown eyes hid themselves away, now belonging to something feral.

'I am here to take you home, back to your family in Portrock,' Olgo said, slowly extending their hand out to the trembling wreck. Tasha flinched at Olgo's touch. Olgo pulled their hand back. Seeing Tasha physically and mentally scarred, possibly for the rest of her life, had turned on something that they couldn't control.

Boupha leant down beside Tasha and put her arm around her.

'We need to get you out of this place, Tasha, and back to your home,' Boupha said in her best child-commanding voice, and it worked. Tasha just did as she was told and stood up with Boupha's support.

'Escort them to a medical centre,' Olgo ordered, trying to keep the tremor out of their voice. 'And then bring them to the ship.'

Olgo turned to Boupha. 'I am in dire need of some resourceful people to replace my operatives. Would you be interested in a job? I can guarantee the pay and conditions are a lot better than what you are used to.'

After a moment's hesitation, Boupha replied. 'Sure.' Her eyes were wide with shock.

'And pick up those two, Suong and Xuan, on your way to the ship, would you?' Olgo asked.

'Are you sure your boss is going to be OK with that?' Boupha asked.

'I have just risen from the dead, my dear. I could get away with murder right now,' Olgo said before turning back to Midas.

'You have all the security personnel here?' Olgo asked.

'Yes, we have a couple of dozen of them in the assembly hall,' Midas replied.

Olgo inhaled deeply, trying to calm their ragged breathing as they watched Boupha and the mechs escort the bundle of flesh and bones that used to be Tasha from the station. Olgo had experienced an emotional rollercoaster since their emcon device had stopped working. But now the rage sent tremors through their bunched up fists.

'She used to play the violin, you know,' Olgo said as they blinked away a tear from their eye.

'It's a shame what they did to her,' Midas said.

'There has been a change of plan,' Olgo growled through gritted teeth. 'Bring the Guild council here.'

'Yes, Ser,' Midas replied as she switched channels to another team member.

She turned and marched off down the hall. Olgo sat down on Tasha's filthy bed, clenching and unclenching their fists on the edge of the mattress.

Somebody had suffered even worse than they had out of this whole mess, never mind their operative and all the Martians that had died at the riot and then in the pit.

Children, even babies. Their chest heaved, and the emotions swarmed in every direction.

But what about Genevieve's instructions? And more importantly, what would happen to Suong if Olgo was fired? But it was too late. Something had broken inside them. Hatred and rage bubbled up from within, like lava spilling out of a volcano. They ground their teeth as they gripped the soiled blankets. The implanted memories of the joy of inflicting pain surfaced and bubbled like a boiling pot of oil.

Midas returned to the open door of the cell.

'Ser, we have them all in the assembly hall.'

Olgo stood up and walked purposefully down the corridor. They stopped at a munitions cabinet and took out one of the infamous Martian bolt guns.

'Show me where,' Olgo ordered.

Midas pointed. Olgo pushed the doors open forcefully and marched in, looking around at the gathered council members and guards. Lisin had certainly lost that stupid swagger.

'Everyone kneel against that wall,' Olgo bellowed with genuine anger for the first time they could remember.

The prisoners looked around, concerned, but they all scrambled to comply as the two mech guards raised their gun arms.

'I thought you said no deaths today, Ser?' Midas questioned.

'I had a change of heart,' Olgo said hoarsely as they walked towards the closest guard. They would leave Garcia and Lisin until last.

EPILOGUE

'I don't know what the hell happened down there. Under normal circumstances, you would be getting shit-canned to whatever level exists below the Basement.'

Even through the basic holo, Olgo could see the venom in those black little eyes.

'But, fortunately for you, the day that changes everything has come. And I need all hands on deck. You will report to the NX. It ships out to the Cold tomorrow. And Olgo, you better keep your shit together this time.'